VILLAIN, SMILING

Edited by Alex Berkman

quercusrubra.co.uk

And I thought: My God... the genius of that! The genius! The will to do that! Perfect, genuine, complete, crystalline, pure... To kill without feeling, without passion, without judgment... without judgment! Because it's judgment that defeats us.

First Document
    1.
    2.
    3.
    4.
    5.
Second Document
Editor's Afterword

First Document

1.

I follow you for fifteen miles today, from your nice big house all the way to work. You wear a dark navy tie and a crisp white shirt and you ignore the car park attendant's friendly greeting just like you always do.

There is no happy ending to this story for you.

I shift my weight and a shirt cuff falls into my face and it makes me jump and I flap at it and kind of puff out my cheeks as if I'm going to blow it away and you stop talking all of a sudden. I wonder if this is it. But no, you just keep talking, and I let out my breath slowly. My ankle is tingling so I stab it with the tip of my knife, I can barely even feel it I've been sitting on the floor in your wardrobe for so long.
Izzie hasn't spoken in over twenty nine minutes and your capacity for talking talking talking continues to surprise me. I don't think I've ever known someone quite as oppressively yet pointlessly verbose as you. On and on and on, an unending droning litany of narcissistic masturbatory verbal diarrhea. Well here's some fucking payback you unbearable bore boor boar.

Ten thousand worse than ever yet I did, Would I perform, if I might have my will; If one good deed in all my life I did, I do repent it from my very soul.

You're my friend on Facebook. You've retweeted my jokes on Twitter four times, favourited seventeen. You've upvoted me on Yik Yak and Reddit and Corlo. You seeded one of my torrents for three weeks and two days, and left eBay feedback for me twice. Your home alarm code is 64275. I've read every email you've sent and received across three accounts (one work, two personal) for eleven months, intercepted every WhatsApp and IM* message for ten and three months respectively. I've hacked your voicemail twice (you forgot your pin sixty days ago). Someone in your company's IT team sends me your browsing history and keylogger data every Friday evening. We've spoken on the phone six times, none of which you'll remember. I've sat near you on the train eight times, and followed you between your home and your office forty-three times. Your phone pin number is 1379. I play computer games with your son every day. You leave your shed unlocked most nights. I have eighteen cameras in your home.

So you want a bit of context. Set the scene, establish motivation, et cetera. I'm watching the telly one stuffy summer afternoon. I'm young, maybe twelve or thirteen. An ad break comes on. New car, supermarket, gravy, new car, chocolate bar. The usual crap. Then, staring out at me, a bunch of starving African kids. Round bellies and big puppy eyes and twiggy arms. Slow motion shots. You know the type. They still show them all the time, these charity appeals, so don't try to tell me you haven't seen them. Then the news comes on and there's another bunch of African kids, top story. But these kids are different. They're not twiggy. Not a potbelly in sight. No, these kids look serious. They look fucking *mean*. Hopped up on drugs, driving down dusty roads in white pickups, shooting up villages with AK47s, feet spread wide apart so they aren't thrown on their backs by the recoil, rat-tat-tat, rat-tat-tat, nice trigger control little man. Forget the bags of rice, forget the two quid a month. They're not waiting around. They're not putting up with the life Ma and Pa have settled for. Fuck being hungry all the time, fuck the face full of flies, fuck the ten kilometre trek for filthy water, fuck the shanty town and the dusty floor and the rags and the fucking misery of it all. Fuck all of that. No, they're taking charge. AK47s all round. *Voila*. No more starving kids. Really quite inspiring if you think about it.

I had a book once, a very long time ago now, dog-eared as anything. The title was *Infamous Serial Killers*. I read it cover to cover as a teenager, over and over and over. I can still remember the red and black front cover, the black and white crime scene photos, vividly. I just have to remember the title and there they all are, as clear as day.

I had plenty of questions, of course. Why were they dissolving bodies in their own basements? Why did they always rape and kill the girl who lived across the road? Why were they taking mementos and tokens and carving their initials and writing letters and revisiting crime scenes and taunting the police? Back then I thought *infamous* meant the opposite of *famous* (what a country), so this was a book about the unsuccessful serial killers. You know, the ones that didn't quite make it to the Hollywood Hall of Fame of Serial Killers, the also-rans, the Sunday morning football ones. I thought somewhere out there was a book called *Famous Serial Killers* with all the really clever ones, the Premiership ones, if you like. The ones that the infamous ones aspired to be, if only they had the smarts. That made perfect sense, given some of the moronic shit the ones in my book pulled. Of course they were *in*famous, half of them must have been technically retarded.

When my stupid adolescent brain figured out what infamous really meant a few years later I was horrified.

It took me a long time to figure out that the clever ones, the really clever serial killers, well they're neither famous or infamous. The best ones? You haven't ever heard of them.

I fucked your wife three times eighty-six nights ago, the second time in her ass, all times without a condom.

You have nobody to blame but yourself. I warned you, didn't I? Twelve months ago to the day that I am writing this, I warned you, yet you did nothing. And like I said before, this does not end well for you.

Your daughter has green eyes.

He's an older guy, perhaps fifty or fifty five. His thick hair is silver and neatly combed away from his forehead. He wears tiny, oval glasses and is peering owlishly at me with barely disguised lust. His eyes flit along the outline of my shoulder and towards my thighs as I grab him a beer from the bucket on the balcony.

We sit for a long time in the light from the streetlamps below. He wets his lips in anticipation. I do the same. I notice his knee bouncing up and down under his corduroy trousers. I take a long sip of beer, draining it, the frothy bubbles dancing on my tongue. I've been in Dortmund nearly five weeks without incident. I'm almost shaking with the excitement of it, the anticipation. *Tonight's the night.*
I'm just about to make my move when I hear the outside door clatter shut below us. I stand up from the sofa, my hand quickly into my pocket, a thumb hovering against the release of the switchblade.
Footsteps on the landing and then Chloe barges through the door, out of breath. She looks at the man for a few seconds, then tells him to verpiss dich. He grunts, rising from the sofa. Chloe and I both watch him as he strides over to her and slaps her across the mouth.
I react fast. The knife is out of my pocket and against the back of his thigh before he can make another move.
I find it interesting the ones that seem to know straight away. Like they can smell it in the air. They know that it isn't just an idle threat, that a few centimetres is all that stands between a nicked femoral and them bleeding out like a stuck pig. My lusty owlish visitor is one of them. He goes very still, his mouth opening and shutting a few times like a fish. Chloe's mouth is bleeding where his slap has loosened a tooth, and I saw her make to spit. The crimson jet lands on the floor, instead of the man's face. Always in control, our Chloe.
Who's this? she asks. I don't answer. The man turns his head a little to the right, trying to look at me over his shoulder. I step closer, making sure he can feel my breath on his neck. Wallet is in my jacket, he says. Maybe he didn't understand after all.
Chloe walks over to the man's jacket and starts rifling through the pockets. She finds the wallet and tosses it onto the table without opening it, then throws his jacket across the room at me. Be more careful next time, she says. I'm not sure which of us she is talking to. Before I can say anything else the bloke turns, grabs his jacket, and runs out the flat, slamming the door behind him. I stand listening as he runs down the stairs and into the street.

Behind me Chloe is gargling from a bottle of vodka, the wallet still untouched where she'd thrown it.
Friend of yours? she asks when I finally realise that the man is gone, escaped, alive. I fold the knife and hold it in front of me, making sure Chloe can see it. But she isn't looking.
I stuff the switchblade back into my trouser pocket, my hands still shaking.
There's a place I know, empty, if you want to take them there. I can show you. Don't bring them here. I have all my shit here.
I look around the flat.
Well, my drink, she says, taking a long swig from the upturned vodka bottle.
I feel like explaining but I don't know how, and the prickling disappointment drains me quickly. I flop down on the sofa next to her and look through the man's wallet, leafing through a few dirty notes before pocketing them.
Messy way to make money, she says, and I think she is joking. But when I look at her face I knew she can smell the hunger on me, knows what that man was here for, what she'd interrupted.
Chloe saw all that. She sat there and looked at me, the *real* me, and took another swig of vodka, a little blood from her mouth backwashing into the clear bottle.
And that's all you need to know about Chloe.

You ever read *The Twits*? Children's book. Dahl is one of my favourite authors. He's got a wicked streak in him, a real streak of sadism, that only people like me can really appreciate. You should go read it now, if you haven't already, but I'll give you a quick rundown assuming you're too busy right now piecing your life back together to read a kid's book.
Well Mr Twit (yes that's his name) lives with Mrs Twit, and they don't get along so well. Can't stand each other, actually. So they play all these tricks on each other, on account of their despising the hell out of one another. So far, so normal as far as kid's books go, right?
But what really gets me is this *one* trick, this one mindfuck that Mr Twit pulls on Mrs Twit. *The Terrible Shrinks*. Most of the other stuff he pulls is kiddie stuff, gross out, worms for dinner,

that kind of thing. But the Terrible Shrinks is a big step up. You know what he does? Every night, for weeks and then months, he attaches little pieces of wood to the feet of Mrs Twit's favourite armchair and the bottom of her walking stick. Now these little bits of wood are so thin that she doesn't notice anything's changed in the morning, at least not at first. It's subtle. And every night Mr Twit goes back, fucking with her, five slivers of wood at a time. Her armchair is getting taller and taller, and her cane is getting longer and longer, but it's all so slow, so incremental, that she never notices a thing, until one day she's walking around with a walking stick above her shoulder and her legs dangling from her chair. It's only then that Mrs Twit clocks on that things aren't quite right. And here comes the best part: Mr Twit convinces the stupid old bag that *she's the one shrinking*. She's got The Terrible Shrinks. Mr Twit persuades her that *she's* the one changing.

Now of course it wouldn't take much for her to realise that wasn't really the case, that he's just fucking with her cane and her chair, but come on, this is a children's book, and Mrs Twit isn't the brightest of the bunch. But it's a pretty good trick if you ignore all that, don't you think?

Mindfucking someone like that over weeks and months, then convincing them that it was *them* changing all along, that it was *their* fault? Imagine the kind of person who lies awake at night coming up with something like that. The kind of person who creeps downstairs every single night for weeks and months to superglue five pieces of wood to the bottom of a chair and a walking stick in the dark while his wife snores upstairs, the kind of person with the patience to cut up all those little bits of wood, to stand there quietly holding the wood against all the other little slivers of wood while the glue dries, polishing and sanding it down to get it just right so she won't notice the join, to get up in the morning and have breakfast with her and not react when he sees that little frown on her face, the kind of person who sees those little acts of clumsiness with this oversized walking stick that his crippled wife needs so badly to walk with and keeps a straight face, the kind of person who notices the barely perceptible lifting of her feet from the floor as she's sitting

watching the telly night after night but doesn't say anything, watching her like she's the frog you cook by turning up the heat and she never has the fucking brains to see she's being cooked one degree at a time until it's finally time to explain it all, to serve the boiled frog, the kind of person who can convince her that she's got that fucking stupid illness that no sane person would ever believe but she does because she has to, there's no other explanation, it can only be one thing, THE TERRIBLE SHRINKS.
Imagine that kind of person for a minute.

You drink too much, and you eat like a pig. Nobody in your office likes you and they talk about you behind your back constantly. Your son never talks about you at school. You spend an average of six minutes a day talking to him, which might surprise you. It sounds like a lot and it is, because most of it is of the Have you got your bag No you can't have that Put that down Stop making that racket Because I said so variety which technically counts but we both know it doesn't. What is your son's favourite Call of Duty map? Name three of his friends. Name two computer games he plays (other than Call of Duty). Name his five favourite Real Madrid players. Name *one*. When was his last parent evening? What position does he play on the football team? Who does he masturbate thinking about at night?
OK the last one was a trick question but you get my point.

Let's talk about your brother, William.
Your brother works for R__ Bank. He's forty-eight. His wife's name is Rachel, but he calls her Rach, which she doesn't like. They have three boys; Luke, Peter, James. They live in a four-bed semi. William drives a BMW 5-series, and he regularly flouts the speed limit. He carries a gold lighter with him in his right jacket pocket, even though he hasn't smoked for fifteen years. Rach(el) cuts five deep incisions on the inside of her thighs about once a month with a sterilized Stanley knife and has done so since she was eleven, or at least that's what she's told her therapist.
Sixty-two days ago I sent your brother five pictures from your email address, __@gmail.com.

One of the pictures is of your daughter in the shower. One is of her sleeping in your living room on a Sunday, the late afternoon sun just catching her bare shoulder. One is of her dancing to Taylor Swift in her bra and pants, her right arm a little blurred but otherwise a perfectly good shot. One is of her crying after Tom, her boyfriend, broke up with her, all big panda mascara eyes. One is of her in her school uniform, a close up of her face as she puts lip-gloss on in the mirror of her bedroom.

Now maybe you're wondering what the normal reaction is for a man who receives an email with five softcore pictures of his fourteen-year-old niece attached with 'Thought Youd Be Interested' as the subject line from his brother, her father? Yes? Well I can tell you. Here's a glimpse into the mind of your brother in the hours after he opened my (your) email, care of his Google search history:

virus protection downloads
email hacking
spyware
child porn laws sentences max UK
child porn categories severity
how to delete hard drive free download
hard drive destruction
magnets buy online
industrial magnets supplier L___
disk wipe
download kill disk
confidential photo printing
password files
secure partition
amazon.co.uk: buy usb

Would you like to know which one of those pictures your brother her uncle opened seventy-three times, with an average viewing time of four minutes eighteen seconds? Or would you like to know which picture he deleted after viewing only five times? The answer may surprise you.

Blackmail. That's the answer to your question. No, not *that* question. The other one. You're a practical man, after all. You want to know the logistics of the thing. Well there you go. Simple. Blackmail. That's how I afford my cameras, the rent on the house across the street and three doors down from your house, how I afford to buy out the cleaning contract from your regular woman Ms Bonczek, the bribes to the alarm company and three security men at your office and your wife's yoga instructor and the Steam and PSN gifts for your son and the GPS trackers and the three vans and motorbike and everything and anything I ever needed during these last twelve months of my campaign.

In the early days it was crude. Chloe had the idea first, and I was only really roped in for the grunt work. It was entrapment, mostly. Narcotic or sexual. As the money began to pour in we expanded into a more sophisticated operation, a more technical setup, if you like. No more buying hookers hoping a CEO would dial her number or roll by her corner in his Mercedes. No more drug deals with the politician's slutty kids. With a regular income we could afford to branch out a bit, and we didn't have to pounce prematurely. I got more involved when I realised how many doors it opened for me. With a bit of security behind us we had enough to squeeze them for *everything*, and it turns out that my hobbies can get pretty expensive, so all that dosh really came in handy.

My personal favourite was using the wife. Chloe preferred the Matrix version of This Is Your Life. Each to their own. The wife was actually one of the cheapest ways, and didn't rely on anything but the distrust you found in any marriage that had pre-nups and trust funds and offshore accounts. It didn't even matter if the husband was an angel when you've got Photoshop and a few cameras in the house to get the right angles. The wives of the rich, the *really* rich, are never the smartest cookies, but they always had access to what really mattered; every digit to their husband's Jersey and Geneva accounts memorised. It was nearly too easy to persuade them that our doctored pictures were the real deal. Depending on the flavour (political, commercial or industrial) we changed them up a bit, sometimes with a dead hooker, other times with an underage boy, wispy moustache included, and even one time with a racing horse named Dancing Queen (the tech had fun doing that one), but always gross or indecent or shocking enough that the wives couldn't look to closely and serious enough that it'd destroy both their reputations and the legal fees would be ruinous to both of them. That was the important bit. It never pays to go too far. You've got to give them an out, make them see that there's a choice, make sure paying is just the least bad option. What's a few grand here and there to those kind of people, anyway?

This is not blackmail, by the way. Let me make that clear. That just pays the bills. I don't want your negotiable bearer bonds. No, this is something altogether more fun.

We first meet on a flight between Frankfurt and Heathrow. You are alone, reading a copy of *The Economist*. You are in the window seat but your ticket is for the aisle, and I hear you convince the old man whose seat you are sitting in that he is reading the sign wrong. You ignore the safety talk by Andi, our elaborately made-up hostess from Liverpool. You buy two small bottles of red wine and a packet of salt and vinegar crisps, even though Andi has to go all the way back to the other cart to get them because they are Out of that particular flavour, sir, but I can check the- and you dismiss her with a flick of the hand and read an article on Indonesian politics whilst she struggles along the aisle against the flow of people heading for a piss and squeezes by the other cart and gives Helene, the other air hostess, her hair coiled tightly and piled up in a knot on her crown like a dog turd, a kind of shrug of the shoulders like she's saying These brutes then she catches my eye as I've turned to watch her and she gives me the smile they teach that means You're a pervert but you're the customer and I wink and look back through the gap between the seats at your knees wedged under the little drop down tray and the two bottles of wine that you've pretentiously left open but not poured like the cretinous man you are as if £5 airline wine needs *airing* and you turn the page before you could have possibly finished reading the Indonesia article and pretend to read an article on a Japanese minister's visit to the Yasukuni shrine, there's a man who knows how to play dirty, a very Japanese way of saying fuck you, and you fail to tip Andi and count the change she gives you back from the twenty you gave her and make sure she sees you doing it before you put the note and coins into your wallet holding it open just far enough so she can see how many other notes are in there but she is already dealing with the next pervert-customer and you prematurely turn the page of *The Economist* again.

No, this did not happen to you because of the way you treated Andi or the old man or for failing to appreciate the well-researched articles in the Asia section of *The Economist* or being pompous about wine or the contents of your wallet. But that was my first impression of you, and I thought you'd like to hear it. Perhaps you remember that flight? Probably not. It was over a year ago. Before that we were two strangers on a plane. You never saw my face. If that had been the only time we'd ever interacted, as much as my staring at your hand and knees through the gap between the airline seats counted as us *interacting*, then maybe none of this would have happened. Or maybe not.

I fly on fake passports, by the way. It's the only way to travel these days. Nice try though. And no, I don't sell soap and you are not Tyler Durden, however much you might like to be.

There's a Saramago book that I forget the name of now about this old clerk who works day in and day out at a registry office, filing and stamping and shuffling and copying birth marriage and death records of his city's inhabitants. It's monotonous work, and the guy has no life whatsoever outside of his job. He even lives in a little apartment attached to the office. He talks to no-one. Despite the drudgery of the work he seems relatively content, if that kind of work-induced stupor can be called contentedness.

Then one day, for no real reason at all, he decides to use his access to the city records to look up some celebrities. Birth dates,

school history, that sort of thing. Pretty innocuous stuff. But he finds something whilst he's hunting into the background of all these other people, these famous and significant people, the kind of people that if you stopped the regular Joe or Jose in the street and you mentioned their names they'd say Oh yes I know her was she really born in X? Did she really flunk Maths? Those kind of people. Important people. Well during this celebrity biographical hunt he stumbles upon this random woman's file. She's a nobody. She's not pretty. Not famous. Not special or particularly interesting. An everybody. A nobody. But for some reason this clerk gets very interested in her. Something about her tickles his fancy. Something that no-one else can see. But he can see it all right. He knows he has to find out everything about her. He tracks down her old school and breaks in to find her school records. He finds out where she's lived, he talks to her former neighbours, acts like an insane person desperately trying to find this woman. The whole time he never questions why he's doing it, what it is about this nobody woman that has piqued his curiosity so much that he's acting completely out of character, completely distracted from his regular work that is his life, breaking into schools and forging official letters and tracking down neighbours and interviewing relatives. Maybe he can't explain it in so many words. Maybe it's like a compulsion. Just one glimpse of that file, one glance at that nobody's face and he's hooked. He has to see it to the end, and fuck the consequences. He has to know everything about this nobody, find out every stupid little detail about her inconsequential life.
He just can't help himself. The nobody fascinates him.

I pay your neighbour Mr Taylor £4100 to buy those chickens, with the stipulation that he procure five roosters and house them next to your wall (they need lots of sunshine, I explain in my best undergraduate). He believes my email about B__ University's Urban Farming trial and spends the money left over from the grant for acquiring, housing, and feeding the chickens on a brand new sound system deal that I'd been spamming his inbox with for months. As you know, Mr Taylor enjoys country and western music, and, at 73, he's a little hard of hearing.

One thing you should know about me: I enjoy the petty shit just as much, if not more, than the serious stuff. Rouse him. Make after him, Poison his delight, Proclaim him in the streets. Incense her kinsmen, And, though he in a fertile climate dwell, Plague him with flies. Though that his joy be joy, Yet throw such changes of vexation on't, As it may lose some colour.

Talking of serious stuff. Your mother. You will never appreciate quite how I enjoyed that one, despite the above disclaimer. I never had a mother growing up so yours became a kind of surrogate for mine, someone for me to take all my anger at the world on.
(That was a lie. Haha.)
Yes, that was me. Of course it was me. There is no such thing as bad luck or coincidence when I have you in my sights.
Are you starting to feel a bit uneasy yet? I mean up until now I could be talking about anyone, this could still be a prank, I could be fucking insane, but now I've mentioned your mother... Maybe what if and I wish I could see your face but maybe I can? Maybe I can.
Of course I can.
Did she tell you about the urn? You never mentioned it, so I suspect she didn't. A shame; that was easily my favourite part.
The superstitious ones are the easiest; the religious a cake walk. I'd only been only living in her loft space for five days before I pulled the urn trick. I waited until she was on the phone again to Mr Anderson. She never found the fishing wire. She surprised me, though. Do you know what she did with your dear old pa's ashes? Hoovered them right up. She was shaking like a leaf, and I thought she was going to shuffle off right there. But for all her frantic hail marys and lord jesuses she hoovered up your old man and emptied him into the black rubbish bin outside like he was no more than a pile of coal ash.
Superstitious maybe, but not sentimental.
And I'll give your Ma some credit. She caught on to the slivers of wood on the end of the cane trick only three days in, chucked it out and got another one from the back of a cupboard. Like I said,

that kind of stuff only works in children's books. Smart lady after all. Smarter than you, anyway.

Do you remember what you said to her on the phone when she told you about his shirts? No, that wasn't the dementia. That was me again. Incidentally, so was the toothpaste, the cat food lasagne, the phone calls, the blood in the toilet and the midnight Sinatra. There were more, plenty more; that's just the highlight reel. So those shirts of his really *were* neatly folded up in the fridge wrapped in tinfoil. And here's what you said when she phoned you up at the end of her tether, the fear of God Almighty in her, the shirts just the last in a relentless campaign to make her lose her fucking mind:

Ma you can't keep phoning me up with this stuff I've got my own problems can't you understand that?

Oh, she understood that all right. Crystal clear sonny jim. If you want anything done in this life you've got to do it yourself.

It woke me up. I crept downstairs from the loft, my stomach growling. It filled the whole house, and it was delicious. I walked into the kitchen and it was like someone was making bacon sandwiches in a hairdressers. It took me a moment to realise what I was seeing. Even these jaded eyes couldn't quite grasp what the soles of those fluffy pink slippers were doing there at that angle. Funny story: I thought for a moment she was cleaning the filthy old thing. I mean, who the hell does it *that* way? Hanging or razors or pills or just a slip in the bath and a few days in hospital with a gammy hip and a nice dollop of MRSA'll do it for most her age. And your old ma had an *electric* oven. Not a gas one. But she made do with what she had like only her generation could.

Your dead mother's roasting head smelled fantastic.

Which was a shame because I had a lot more lined up for her. But you won't catch me complaining. She didn't even have to tie herself to the thing. No, really, *think* about that for a minute. She lay there and took it. I've nothing but admiration for that kind of willpower. That *determination.* She grit those pristine dentures of hers and forced herself to sit through it before she passed out, and I never heard a peep.

So I'm not moaning. Anything but. Besides, that loft was dusty as hell. And the look on her face when I pulled the fish wire and broke the urn and scattered the ashes over that horrendous lime green carpet the precise moment she was telling randy old Mr Anderson the colour of her knickers (pink) was, I must say, fucking priceless. I don't think I could have topped that even if I'd been in her loft a month.

And yes, I know what you're thinking. The note. That was me as well. She didn't have the time or the inclination, chased into the hellfire of that fan-assisted electric oven by the ghost of her old man. You should have realised that. Old lady handwriting my speciality (Not really. I faked it. Computers.) THE LAST WILL AND TESTAMENT OF A_ _. The North American Man/Boy Love Association would have used the money much better than you. How much did you spend contesting it again? (Don't tell me. I know.)

You should ask Mr Anderson about the silver dining set, if you get the chance. That actually wasn't me for once.

Here's a good question for you. Can you spot the odd one out: Ingrid Bergman, Amélie, the Manson family, or the East German Stasi?

Give up?

Here's a clue. *Zersetzung*. Better known to you and me as gaslighting, and even more commonly known as mindfucking someone with petty tricks like moving their furniture or switching their shoes or changing their profile picture or spiking their drinks over a prolonged period in order to disturb them enough that they become convinced they're losing their marbles or that their dead husband is haunting them from beyond the grave for giving arthritic handjobs to Mr Anderson.

Poor Ingrid Bergman was a victim of zersetzung, whilst Amélie, the Manson family and the Stasi were all enthusiastic perpetrators, to varying degrees.

Ingrid Bergman found[1]

Sweet, quirky Amélie! She spots a grotesque greengrocer exploiting a touched crippled but sweet young man, and she decides to teach him (the greengrocer not the retard) a lesson or two. Cue the accordion. She's crafty. She sneaks into the greengrocer's house (so much easier when you have they key). She switches his slippers out for a smaller pair, cuts his shoelaces, replaces his toothpaste with foot cream, reverses the door handles, fucks with his alarm clock, replaces his light bulbs, unplugs his bedside lamp and sticks a pin through the wire so when he comes to plug it back in it'll blow the fuse. All very zersetzung. Small, subtle changes, one sliver of wood at a time. Insignificant pranks, minor inconveniences on their own, but together, together they make you start to question *everything*. That's the beauty of zersetzung. You're never quite sure what is real or not. You feel persecuted, victimised, but there's no-one to blame but yourself.

The nasty greengrocer gets back home after a long day of selling cabbages and he doesn't notice a thing, at first. But the next morning his alarm wakes him up hours too early and we see him discovering all of Amélie's cute little tricks one-by-one, and all through the rest of the day he's left asking himself What the hell is going on? What could go possibly go wrong next? It's exhausting, that constant nagging worry, and by the end of the day he's pretty fucking upset. He's sitting looking around his house with this half-afraid half-bemused look on his face, and you can see him starting to question his sanity. He remembers all the weird, inexplicable changes. The *bad luck*. He's never experienced anything like it. He has no idea about Amélie, no idea that someone might be playing trick after trick on him, because Why? What has he done in this life to be plagued by such petty pranks like sliced shoelaces or foot cream for toothpaste? Such a thing is incomprehensible to imagine. No

---

[1] Editor's Note: The author left this sentence unfinished in the original document. Ingrid Bergman played the character of Paula in George Cukor's movie *Gaslight* (1944). Paula is subject to prolonged psychological abuse at the hands of her husband in an attempt to institutionalise her, including the (unintentional) dimming of gas lights, where this form of mental abuse takes its name.

sane person could imagine such a campaign. Any normal person with a grudge against him would just shout in his face, maybe punch him in the nose. Not break into his house and move shit around, not this *petty* shit, this madness by a thousand pranks. No, there's only one explanation: he's going insane. He's got the phone in his lap, and he's trying to work out what he's going to say, how to make someone believe him, how to get someone tell him that everything's alright, he's not going batshit, he's just having a shitty day. Just like your old Ma wanted from you when she rang. Only when he presses the speed dial for his mother's place it puts him through to a psychiatric helpline. Amélie has reprogrammed the phone, of course. He really starts to sweat then, and there's this sound of birds getting louder and louder and he stumbles over to the liquor cabinet and pours himself a stiff one but our dear Amélie thought of that too, she's a smart little sociopath, and he spits out the salted brandy all over the camera.
Fin.

The Manson family weren't quite as sophisticated as Amélie. They went on what they called creepy crawls, a name straight out of a Dahl children's book. They snuck into people's houses out there in LA and rearranged furniture and stole money to fuck with people. Of course, they did a whole lot more than that, but I don't really have time to go into the Manson's I'm sure you can look it up if you want to know more and to be honest the Mansons aren't all that interesting to me.

Now the Stasi? The Stasi could really appreciate the value of a good old fashioned gaslighting zersetzung mindfuck. And just like all totalitarian states, when it came to fucking with people they were really very good at it. Masters, even. I consider myself a student of their methods, honed and perfected on all those liberal playwrights and authors and activist-types behind the Curtain back in the day.
I know what you're thinking. Why are the Stasi wasting time gaslighting their enemies? Why not just string them up, disappear them? Oh, but this is the eighties, and everyone's

pretending like everything behind the Curtain is hunky-dory, A-OK, and vanishing dissidents just isn't politically fashionable. But these pesky fuckers keep scribbling their screeds, bitching and moaning and protesting and whining, and the Stasi need them to can it. So they have to do things on the hush hush, plausible deniability and all that. They have to use those brutal imaginations of theirs and come up with something altogether more interesting.

The first thing before you start a really good zersetzung campaign is to study the potential victim closely. The Stasi were well resourced in this field, so they followed their bitching poet everywhere he went, dug around in his rubbish bin, intercepted his post, tapped his phone, watched where he drank, who he talked to, where he stuck his dick and where he bought his black market fags. You know the drill. A fact-finding mission, an analogue doxxing, if you like. The trick is to find things to exploit. Weaknesses, secrets, traits, passions, interests, fetishes, that kind of thing.

Then they got to work on their poet, and it was usually toe-curlingly fantastic.

I don't have time to go into every detail, it's all there if you want to look it up, but do you want to hear the one thing that made me fucking wet my pants when I first heard about it? Oh sure there's plenty of rearranging furniture and messing with the tea bags and sending vibrators through the post. But my absolute favourite trick? They snuck into one victim's loft and left a fucking X-RAY MACHINE in there. There it sat, churning out radiation into the house below, all day all night. How good is that? Sure, you can mess with a man's mind, fuck around with his stuff, with his friends, with his job, with his family, until he's questioning everything he thinks he knows about the world, but to give him fucking brain cancer at the same time? That is some next level skulduggery.

Really quite inspiring.

(Unfortunately it turns out X-Ray machines are rather hard to get hold of these days.)

I'm watching you and I suddenly have to swallow down the bile as you carry on like normal, drink your stewed tea, stare at the TV, entranced by the moronic moving pictures, and you have no idea, no idea at all that someone can hate you as much as I do right now in this moment and it takes every last fucking bit of willpower for me to stay in my chair, stay away from you, I want so badly to put my fist through your guts and fuck your skull and tear your ugly nose from your face with my teeth and squeeze your heart with my bare hands until my knuckles pop and your teeth shatter

I hit Chloe just once. A sweeping backhand that caught her just under her chin. I broke three teeth and they had to clamp her jaw shut for three weeks. The first thing she did after picking herself up off the floor is spit out her broken teeth into her palm. The next thing she did? She gave me this look. She looks right at me, blood pouring from her mouth, already swelling up, and I just feel the rage drain right out of me like someone pulled the plughole, and I get this feeling in my gut. There's something in her eyes and we both know that's the last time I'll ever hit Chloe again. It turns out we were right. After that, we've never had any problems. We're like family, now, a rock solid partnership, a regular Adolf and Joseph, Frank and Jesse, Fred and Rosemary, Leopold and Loeb, Myra and Ian, Bonnie and Clyde et cetera.

So we're getting off the plane and you ignore Andi as she wishes you a good morning and we're out in the chilly air and I'm right behind you. Neither of us are carrying any hand luggage and we head to the bus and get on and I'm still not really paying much attention to you because I'm here for a completely different reason and it's been a long time since I was back home and I'm having some mixed emotions about it so you are only on the periphery of what I'm paying attention to.
It's the end of half term and there are lots of kids on the flight and they take a long time getting off the plane and onto the bus. You are playing on your phone and looking up every now and again and if you had a watch you'd have checked it four or five times but you don't so you make do by making these little

huffing sounds and I'm starting to get a bit more interested in you. The bus is starting to fill up and soon there's no seats left and we're both sitting down and a flustered looking Mom comes on dragging two little boys behind her and her eyes are looking around the bus trying to find somewhere to sit but there's no more room, standing room only, and the bus doors close and she needs to sit down as the bus lurches away from the plane. Then you notice a pretty young girl a few seats down looking at you, maybe seventeen or eighteen, and you say too loudly to the Mum, Would you like to sit here, and you make a big show of insisting and you flash a big smile and make sure everyone sees your What A Great Guy act but the teenager isn't looking at you anymore and so you start huffing a bit and you go back to looking at your phone. Then your phone rings and you answer it and I learn one of three things about your wife:
She's stupid
She knows you're a liar
She's both stupid and knows you're a liar
You say I'm sorry honey but I'm still stuck in Frankfurt, and the frazzled Mum looks at you with a What are you talking about you lying liar we're at Heathrow on the bus to the terminal not in Frankfurt look, but you blank her and say, Well you'll have to take him, what can I do about it here? What do you want me to say Izzie? and then because of where I'm sitting I see on the display Call Ended but you say, OK excellent I look forward to it too quickly to nobody and swipe right too many times as if you're the one ending the call but I know that you're not.
So now I'm interested but I'm still not *that* interested, but we're close. Another tosser brushing off his missus to fuck his mistress, big deal, nothing to see here folks but then you keep looking at the teenager and she's getting uncomfortable and I'm enjoying it because you don't seem to get the hint or maybe you do and you don't care and then one of the frazzled Mum's kids knocks into your shin and I can see by the face you pull that it actually hurt and you mutter Cunt under your breath just loud enough for the boy and his Mum to hear and she looks up at the other people standing around and none of them do or say anything about it, they pretend like they didn't hear a thing though by the way they

flinched they did, and her eyes go all glassy and she turns away and the teenager gives you this look but you're looking at the terminal doors that we're approaching and now I'm interested.
Now I'm interested.
Now I'm interested.

My favourite serial killer? I change my mind on this all the time. You know how it is. The South Americans are up there, definitely, purely on the strength of numbers. I guess Gary Ridgway gets an honourable mention, sure. But at the moment I'm leaning towards Yang Xinhai. Go look him up on Wikipedia.
Now I know what you're thinking. Him? Some loser from China? Oh, but wait a second. Scroll down a bit. Here you go:
"When I killed people I had a desire. This inspired me to kill more. I don't care whether they deserve to live or not. It is none of my concern... I have no desire to be part of society. Society is not my concern."
Edgy stuff, right?
Just kidding. It's Bundy, of course.

So it's two days later and you're in town with your family in Pizza Express. You look tired. You're wearing the same shirt as you wore the day before with the too-small collar. It's Saturday, and the restaurant is packed and you're looking like you're regretting ever agreeing to coming out shopping but you needed some more work shoes and if you left it up to Izzie she'd get the wrong damn ones.
The restaurant's small and cramped and it's six o'clock and the place is full. They're queuing out the door, turning people away. It's hot as your Ma's oven will be in a few months' time and you forgot to put deodorant on and there's a wet patch crawling up from your ass crack up along your spine and every time you lean back you feel it sticking against the back of the chair and the beer is lukewarm and five times as expensive as if you bought it from Tesco and the place is swarming with birthday parties and kids and noise and the waitress still hasn't come to get your order and some cunt keeps popping balloons and you are kind of scowling already.

The day before I sent your daughter three links on Instagram and she clicked them all and now I can see everything she does on her phone. So that morning I sent her five PETA videos from one of her friends and she watched them all and I smile when I hear her ask the waitress (she has to shout) for the vegetarian pizza and the waitress smiles back at her and says Sure hun you want cheese on that? Then you sort of explode out of your chair and everyone sees you order a Sloppy Giuseppe for your teenaged daughter like some Muslim autocrat and a Dad at the next table laughs because the way you phrased made it sound like you were asking the fat waitress to perform a sex act and your daughter is shouting back at you about antibiotics and slavery and Izzie is just doing this strange little head wobble and saying nonononono and then you pick up the bottle of warm beer and you throw it at the laughing Dad's head and you're a bad aim and I can't stop laughing and I pop another balloon and your face is unforgettable as the big Polish chef comes out from behind the counter carrying a pizza cutter his forehead glistening with sweat and you leave but your daughter stays at the empty table with the waitress who's giving her a drink and then sits down next to her with her chubby arm around her delicate bare shoulders but you don't look back and then you're gone and then I know, I know, you're absolutely the one for me.

I love reading about medieval torture methods online. It's like The Twits but real life. I like to imagine the brainpower that went into thinking some of those things up. My favourite? That's an easy one. Chinese water torture. Here's what Wikipedia says:
"Victims were strapped down so that they could not move, and cold or warm water was then dripped slowly on to a small area of the body; usually the forehead. The forehead was found to be the most suitable point for this form of torture because of its sensitivity: prisoners could see each drop coming, and after long durations were gradually driven frantic as a perceived hollow would form in the centre of the forehead."
I like that. *A PERCEIVED HOLLOW.* That part always makes me smile.

Oh, where to start. There have been so many. So many countless slivers, so many countless straws, so many countless cuts, it's nearly impossible for me to remember them all. I'll have to check back through the files.

I sent bad racist jokes by text to your father-in-law from you. He didn't know how to react to this new line of communication I've opened so he sits very quietly expecting you to tell them to his face when they came over every Sunday for dinner so your mother-in-law takes up the conversational slack and if there's anything you hate worse than your father-in-law's lectures it's your mother-in-law's inane ramblings about cookery shows. You won't say anything to your wife because they're old and a little overweight and they have a big house in O_ and a place outside of Marseilles and you look at it as an investment, time served.

Drip.

I deleted every thirteenth email you received from your boss before it ever reached your inbox. You didn't realise because you never pick up the phone or walk twenty metres to his office because you hate having to kiss his ass all the time because you're not very good at your job.

Drip.

I gave £100 and an It's For His Own Good cold turkey talk to Tom, your Starbucks barista, to make your regular morning latte-to-go decaf. I only asked him to do it for two weeks but he still does it because you speak to him like he's a piece of shit.

Drip.

I left pictures you took of Izzie lounging around on a topless beach in Spain in your son's room. He looked at them for twenty-three minutes before he masturbated. The second time he masturbated he was wearing a pair of her pants that I didn't know he had, which fit his slim, twelve-year-old hips surprisingly well. Izzie must have put on a lot of weight since he stole them. You kept the pictures even though Izzie told you to get rid of them.

Drip.

You yell when you talk on the phone. You also type really fucking loud, like you've got it in for your keyboard, as if it was somehow responsible for your mother topping herself or your daughter being a vegetarian or your wife never putting out. So I replaced your keyboard with a custom one that looks exactly the same but which randomly spews out letters you haven't pressed every now and again. As you're a moron and incapable of typing without watching your fat fingers stabbing at the keys, you only notice later on when you reach the end of a paragraph, and it drives you insane and makes you bash the keys even more loudly. Your secretary, Eliza, who sits in the adjacent office, despises you for this, and she routinely forgets to pass on your messages. You never ask Eliza about her daughter or her weekend plans.

Drip.

I sent a bizarre, threatening, anonymous letter to E_ K_ Systems, the biggest client in your portfolio, that only you could have sent. That was why they decided to end their association with your company, for a loss of business worth about £7m a year. I sent your line manager an email from E_ K_ Systems raising their suspicions about your involvement. You won't be considered for promotion again until 2024, at the earliest, according to your HR file. You blamed a junior colleague, Frank, for the loss of the contract.

Drip.

I replaced the aspirin you took every morning with dextroamphetamine. Zing. When you started taking them in the evening I replaced them with a mixture of zolpidem and benzodiazepine. Yawn. As far as I know, you're still taking them. No one's making you.

Drip.

All that dripping reminds me of that urban legend. I bet you know what I'm talking about, but I'll tell you anyway because maybe you don't and it's a good story (I prefer the one with the doll though, or maybe the psycho with the hook for a hand; it's a close call).
So a young girl is home alone. Maybe she has green eyes, maybe she doesn't. Her parents have gone out (separately); her Dad to fuck his mistress, and her Mum to be fucked by me three times (one time in the ass, no times with a condom).
It's getting late, and the maybe-green-eyed girl decides she's had enough of watching the TV and she goes upstairs to her room for a wank. So up she goes, and the family dog, Harriet, trots up with her. Well anyway maybe-green-eyes plays with herself for about eighteen and half minutes, whispering dirty words under her breath even though her brother is at a sleepover and nobody but Harriet should be able to hear her. About seven minutes after she's finished she falls asleep.
Now a few more minutes later, let's say twenty-three, maybe-green-eyes wakes up. What's that she says to herself. There's like a dripping noise from down the hall. Sounds like a tap dripping in the bathroom she says to herself and she reaches down to stroke Harriet for comfort, because she's a bit scared being in the big house by herself and knowing the dog is there makes her feel safer. She feels the dog lick her hand and there you go, she feels better already. She giggles and says Stop it Harriet but the dog tastes the cunt juice still on her hand and it keeps on licking and by now the maybe-green-eyed-girl is going back to being scared and I'm supposed to stop like in the story where we do this three or four times before she gets up and realises but her hand tastes so good and the dripping keeps going louder and louder and she rushes out of her room toward the bathroom and she opens the door and Harriet is strung up dead and the dripping sound is the dog's blood oozing from its slit throat into the bathtub and when

she goes back to her room she sees scrawled on her wall in dog's blood HUMANS CAN LICK TOO and then she passes out and when she wakes back up her Mum and Dad are back and Harriet has run off and the wall's clean and there's no blood anywhere and she's too scared to say anything and Dad is yelling at her for leaving the back door open and Now that stupid mutt will never come back and I'm back outside in my van listening and laughing and I can still taste fish on my lips.

Wait wait wait. I know, I know. How can I be fucking your wife in the ass AND under the bed licking your daughter's pussy hand? Well that's what we call a dilemma. I guess you'll just have to believe whichever version of the story you prefer. Real life is like that, sometimes. I may have changed the details of the urban legend a bit too but it's there online if you want to look it up.

Your son is very good at FIFA. I bet you didn't know that. Just this evening he's beaten me three times, and I consider myself a pretty good player. And no, I wasn't going easy on him. He won it fair and square, 4-2 - Real vs. Barcelona, so if anything I should have won it. Then we had Big Macs and he said you didn't ever let him eat Maccy D's and I said, Oh really? and he said, Yeah and he doesn't like football or PlayStation either and I said, So it isn't so bad here after all and he just kind of shrugged and dipped his salty fries in the ketchup and stuffed them in his mouth and I felt like fucking Hook and I almost did a Dustin Hoffman impression right there on the spot BUT DID HE GO TO YOUR BASEBALL GAME? All I need is the little wig for him, haha. But seriously you really should have done a better job of raising your kids. One playing FIFA with a serial killer and the other... Anyway he's calling for me so better go put him to bed it's almost 11.30 anyway whatever will his parents say JACK, YOU *ARE* HOME hahaha.

Drip. Humans can lick too. NOW YOU'RE INTERESTED.

2.

So by now you're thinking What the fuck is this? How can this be for real? And you're trying to remember back. You know all too well how hard this past year has been but surely there's no way there's no possible way and you're in denial but at the same time you're doubting yourself because Hold on a minute some of this makes sense Wait a fucking minute I knew something was going on I thought I was going crazy Who the fuck are you you fucking cunt When I find you and you're going all Liam Neeson and there you are you're through the denial and blossoming into anger and you're so pretty when you're angry darling but now you're rereading the bits about your son and your daughter and maybe you're getting a bit scared because Wait a minute. *Wait a minute.* Maybe this isn't some crazy person and maybe just maybe I'm in real fucking trouble here and now you get it.

Let's talk about Izzie.
I made a cheap crack about her earlier. You know, about her being a bit larger than she used to be. Come on I know you remember. It was when I was talking about your son masturbating to that photo of her bare tits while he was wearing her frilly pants. Remember? Anyway, I feel bad about it. No really, I do.
I preferred following Izzie to work because she didn't speed. She drove a blood red Audi A3, and she had it cleaned every Monday so it always shone bright as she pulled into the car park underneath her office building. Dazzling it was. Really popped out. She worked in a nicer part of town than you. You could see her office from right across the street, all glass and bright lights and potted plants and open plan. So *modern*. Well you've been there so you know what I'm talking about. You could sit in the Costa or the empty office on the fourth floor across the street or just in your van in the multi-storey and look right at her all day every day and there she'd be sat, working away, taking phone

calls, joking around with Dan and Martin and Brian and Leo and Richard and all the others she liked to joke around with at work and wherever else you might like to have a joke around, maybe the bar three streets over after work or the hotel right next door after the bar or maybe just a quick joke around in the disabled toilet on the fifth floor of that nice modern office. Just kidding. Izzie didn't fuck around at work, at least I never saw her anyway. Izzie was 153cm (5ft 1in you pleb) tall and had no piercings and yellowy brown hair and she wore Body Shop perfume and liked Game of Thrones and she would have got all my references because she loved movies couldn't get enough of them and she preferred briefs and sensible flat shoes and had a crush on Tom Hardy and her favourite colour was yellow and her favourite flowers were daisies and you bought her zero daisies ever and she said For all intensive purposes when she meant For all intents and purposes and when she talked on the phone she always closed her eyes and she had a fungal infection on her right pinkie toe and she left her hair in the sinkhole and ate peanut butter sandwiches without a plate and she shaved her cunt every Sunday afternoon and she was self-conscious about her ears and had a phobia of spiders and she was a little bit homophobic but she did her best not to show it she was just brought up that way and she always hated your mother and the password to her email was wonderwall77 and fuck you for making me talk about her in the past tense.

As I was writing that bit about Izzie I see on the news another kid has shot up a school. I watch the videos from the circling helicopters and I have to stop myself from shouting out loud at the telly because otherwise I'll wake your kids. But I just can't help it. These American kids make me so fucking angry. They have access to an arsenal beyond my wildest teenage wet dreams and what do they do with them? Go to school. Like they do every fucking day. Zero imagination. I'm feeling really angry today hey you know what Chad What's that Brad Let's go shoot up something Oh good idea Brad where'd you have in mind we can go anywhere we like I guess because we're about to die anyway Oh I tell you what What Let's go to school Great idea my friend really original I like it they'll never expect us there haha we'll really show them Yeah bro lets go but make sure you don't aim for the head or anything you know we wouldn't want to kill more than four or five of them Right you are Chad I probably shouldn't bring any of my grenades or anything then Nah bro probably not OK see ya later on the bus Yeah bro peace out.

Why don't they hit up a toy shop or an old people's home or a strip club or a traffic jam? Hell, go the fucking mall. Mix it up. Anywhere but the one place they go day in day out. Soft targets. Shooting up a school is like walking into a damned army base. If you're wanting to commit mass murder don't go to the one place they're *ready* for you. That's like those cunts who chop up their neighbours. IF YOU'RE FEELING HOMICIDAL DRIVE TO THE NEXT TOWN AT LEAST. Is that really so difficult to understand?

But like I tell the television if you absolutely have to go to school call in bomb threats to five other schools, head to the gymnasium, lock the doors behind you, use BURST FIRE, and always check under the dead teachers (they like hiding there).

Amateurs. I turn the TV off and go back to watching you. At least sometimes you makes sense.

So we've gone this whole time and I bet I know what you're thinking. Was she in on it all along? It's like Rashomon and you're not sure of anything except your wife fucked another guy. Well keep reading and you'll soon find out.

You haven't done anything exciting for a while and since I turned the telly off I was just looking back through my files and I found one called SLENDER and I almost fell off my chair laughing when I opened it up and I saw the pictures again. I'd almost forgotten all about it. So much has happened I sometimes lose track of how far we've come, forget all the good times in our little campaign. Do you remember the camping trip? I bet you do. What a *disaster* that turned out to be. Poor Izzie. No seriously what a shame. You've got to feel sorry for her. She hoped it might bring you back together again after all the shit you'd been through that year (hahaha). Mend a few wounds. Fat chance. You screw it all by being yourself like always.

You ever heard of Slender Man? It's a creepy story that went the rounds on the internet a few years ago. Slender Man is this thin faceless guy in a suit that's been photoshopped into a few blurry pictures. He likes stalking and abducting people, and his favourite prey are white American kids. Now you'd think in this internet age of 4chan and goatse that Slender Man might be a bit fucking scarier than *that*, but I guess it's a generational thing. The kids seem to find it creepy. A couple of them living out in Bumblefuck USA actually stabbed their friend to death because they thought it'd please him.

I know, right?

So Slender Man isn't exactly the scariest thing I've ever heard but when you're twelve years old and you hear it for the first time and you haven't built up any immunity to that kind of thing because your Dad won't let you watch horror movies I guess it might freak you out. Especially when you hear the story three days before you're about to go camping in the middle of fucking nowhere and your Dad thinks it's about time you had your own tent not because you're ready or anything, he just wants to try to fuck your Mum (she wouldn't let him), and to be honest although you're twelve you sometimes act like you're only eight or nine and you still wet the bed (that's an early sign of a serial killer so I'll remember to keep a close eye on that for you). So when a friend you play Call of Duty with sends you an IM with a link about Slender Man and you open it and see the photos and read some of the stories the back of your neck just crawls and you can't stop thinking about it and you wake up eight times in three nights and you won't can't mustn't sleep without the light on else *he'll get you.*

And that's why he really didn't want to sleep in that tent on his own, and that's why he set fire to his pillow. Not because he could hear Izzie rebuffing you in the other tent. Not because he hated you or because you didn't want to play frisbee with him or you forgot the ketchup and the charger for his PSP. Because he was frightened of the dark and of Slender Man who lives in the woods and the only thing the reptile part of his brain could think of that would keep away the monsters was FIRE Just a small one I'll keep this bottle of water with me but then there was smoke everywhere and it was in his eyes and he couldn't see and Mum is screaming and Dad is kicking down the tent. That's why he kept calling you Slender Slender Slender you really should have caught on sooner but you didn't and you just stood there looking at his half-burned tent listening to your son blubbering against his mother's shoulder his pants sopping with piss and you look lost, completely lost, like you didn't know where or who you were and for a minute there you looked like you actually understood, you could feel the hollow forming.

You walked right by my hammock by the way. You were within maybe ten metres of me and you looked right at me but you didn't see me you didn't see me because you're not the real Slender Man.

I just looked it up those American kids did stab their friend for Slender Man, but she didn't die. Amateurs.

I'm in your kitchen with my hand on the lid of the ground coffee when I hear your son shuffling up to the front door, his keys jangling. He's early, too early, and you won't believe this but I actually get a little stab of worry for him. Can you believe that? I'm actually concerned about the little man. I've been chatting with him for so long that my first thought as he's about to find me standing in his kitchen isn't panic, my eyes aren't looking for the back door, my feet aren't propelling me through the window, my hand isn't dropping the coffee and going for the knife rack, oh no, none of that. I'm thinking Why's he home so early what's happened how did he get home which bus did he get did something happen at school is he alright? Now think about that for a second. And now remember back to *your* first reaction when Izzie called you up and told you he'd walked out of class and been suspended. It wasn't How did he get home is he alright is he okay? it was That little shit why is he always doing this. Those were your exact words I can send you the mp3 if you want proof.
I hide in the pantry with the boxes of cereal and the cans of baked beans and I wait until I hear the FIFA commentary drifting

down the stairs before I put the coffee away and sneak out the back and head over to number 63. I was worried for him but I'm not stupid. I wasn't *that* worried. I just remembered it and thought it was a funny story you'd like to hear.

Your mother's funeral is a grand affair. Precisely the kind of thing she would have hated. No small church service presided over by nice Pastor John, family and close friends only with a small buffet at the Memorial Hall afterwards. Oh no. You had to expunge that guilt. The whole thing is costing you £18,350.
You didn't invite Mr Anderson but he shows up anyway. I left out his letters for you to find. That kinky shit he wrote was pretty good, right?
I'm hoping you're about to make a scene. I watch your face closely from the back of the church. You disappoint me. All you do when horny Mr Anderson gets to you in the line is refuse to shake his wrinkly lecherous hand but Izzie and your brother do and no-one notices the slight except Mr Anderson. Like I said, not all of my plans work out. I was convinced you'd punch him in that granny-grabbing mummy-munching lecherous mouth of his but maybe being in that big church next to the vicar and the fact that it was Mr Anderson who found your crispy Ma in the oven held you back.
I have to stifle a laugh when the doddering pastor starts talking about the terrible accident and then again a bit later when he talks about her two dedicated, loving boys and I'm looking at the back of your head and I realise I'm the only one in the whole church who knows who you really are, what you're really like, how much of a kind and doting son you were when she told you there was something supernatural terrorising her like the fucking Poltergeist and you told her you had your own problems to deal with.
Even though the main event is lacking the frisson a fistfight with a pensioner would have had I'm looking forward to the supporting act. Right on cue, they turn up. There are three of them and they look fantastic. I mean perfect. I saw one of them on Newsnight years ago arguing as passionately as someone like him could about lowering the age of consent to twelve. He

backed it up with a whole load of statistics about royal marriages and Medieval customs and even went off on a tangent about Romans and Lucretius before the interviewer cut him off. He's put on a lot of weight since his first and final TV appearance but he's still wearing the same rectangular seventies glasses and even though he's thirty metres away from where I'm sitting I know precisely how he smells, sour milk and week old cat litter and mouldy bread that's been sat in the kitchen for god knows how long wedged in behind the microwave and fridge. Well you saw him so you know what I mean. Could you smell him and his fermenting friends? You were closer to the door after all. Is that why you turned around before they'd even started? Or did you only smell him later, in the excitement that followed?

The international chapter of the North American Man/ Boy Love Association are in good voice that Friday morning and I suspect but can't confirm they'd been drinking, which makes them impervious to all but the strongest headlock. Their protest is brief but they've made their point. They've paid their respects to one of their own, someone who couldn't live in a world where the law dictated who could and couldn't love one another, someone who on her death bed saw the light and was willing to give her hard earned money to their cause, someone who knew that in Jesus's time it was perfectly acceptable if a Man and a Boy felt very deeply and I'm glad they're shouting so loudly because I can't stop laughing and luckily I manage to slip outside through the other door before anyone notices me.

I drive to the hospital in my van and sit in the car park. It relaxes me. The patients aren't allowed to smoke inside the hospital. They give them nicotine patches. But there's always a few who just can't help themselves. A certain type. You know the kind of person I'm talking about. Oh come on don't pretend you don't. They wander off the wards and huddle around the bus shelter. I always park right across from them and keep the engine running and the heat blasting. They come out in their slippers and dressing gowns. Their faces are all gaunt and scabby and feral, their bony fingers curled around their roll ups like something out of Macbeth. Their witchy frog eyes look at me and I look back

and they see the wolf at the door they know it's coming but they don't know how close it is but I do. I can see it on them. I can see the cold burning them all over but they can't help themselves. Drawn out into the dark and the wet and the cold and the pain, picked out in the headlights, stared at by the gawping bus passengers, but there's nowhere else to go. They're like zombies shuffling around in their nighties and they can't help themselves. No one's making them do it. I watch them and I see it all and it just makes my mouth water to see how wretched their lives are how they just can't help themselves. They just can't help themselves.
They remind me of you.

So then you phone your daughter and her phone goes straight to voicemail and you pretend like that doesn't matter and you leave her a message and then you ring her again and it goes straight to voicemail again and then maybe you're getting a bit worried isn't she supposed to be with her Aunt S_? so you ring her but there's no answer because your sister-in-law is at the police station giving a statement No officer I never saw a thing one minute she was in her room the next she was gone and the officer says Did you see anyone suspicious about the premises and she says What do you mean suspicious and he says You know unusual activity, people coming to the door, strangers, workmen, foreigners and the other officer in the room kind of rolls her eyes and drinks her coffee leaving a brown lipstick mark on the rim and your sister-in-law frowns for a second and then says Well there's been a van parked across the road but I never thought anything of it until right this moment when you asked and the woman officer says And where is the missing girl's mother and your sister-in-law says Oh I'm just looking after them until she's back she's at a conference you see with her firm she's a very successful woman and the racist officer says Oh really and she says Yes really.
And then you think No if anything has happened to them your son's school would have rung but they have rung and your secretary Eliza forgot to pass on the twelve messages because Fuck you you want to talk about stress mister I'll give you stress

my daughter has bone cancer and you've never asked me once about it you fat fingered fuck I hope you rot in hell and your daughter's been kidnapped by white slaver sex predators and then you're trying to find the school's number in your phonebook but you don't have it and you call through to Eliza but she's joking around in the disabled toilet with Lee and Paul so you have to Google the school's number and then your phone rings and it says Hello may I please speak to Mr _ and your stomach kind of lurches and you say Yes? and they say Are you the husband of Mrs _? and you think nonononono there's no way it hasn't even been two days and she wasn't supposed to be back from the conference until Thursday but then the voice says I'm afraid I haven't been able to get through to your wife and she's listed as an emergency contact but since I'm talking to you sir well sir its your son sir and you say What about my son and your phone says He's missing sir run off we think and you say Run off and your phone says Well maybe we better talk about it at the station sir there's some things about it we can't quite understand and you say What things and your phone says Just some irregularities sir if you come down to the station I'm sure we can work it all out.
Or something like that, anyway. I wouldn't know. I don't think real cops say things like sir and irregularities, to be honest. I was too busy to listen to the recording. Your daughter is a real squirmer.

You get off the airport bus and you leave behind an unpleasant stench and the Mom is still close to tears. I follow you through customs and I watch you waiting for your bags and I stare at your face for about five minutes until I know every single detail of it. You don't notice me because you're staring at the screen above the carousel. You smile and look around when the alarm sounds as if you are trying to take credit for it moving because you stared at the screen the whole time but no-one is looking at you except me. You watch the bags come out with hungry eyes. You keep standing there even though there's not much room and your bag hasn't come yet and a lady is struggling to get her massive suitcase off the carousel right in front of you but you just look through her you've only got eyes for your bag and there it is coming around the corner professional, black, expensive-ish and you take it and I follow you outside to the taxi and I walk next to you as you lean in through the window. You shout when you see he's Asian because you think he doesn't speak English but of course he does and now half the taxi rank including me know you're going to E_ Street and I go back inside quickly and pick up my keys at the rental desk and I beat you to E_ Street by five minutes because the guy speaks perfect English and he doesn't like you one bit or maybe I just know a faster route than the GPS I don't know. You tell him to wait and you walk to the garage (yes I know about the garage). I'm about as interested now as I've ever been in anyone. Then you spoil it when you come back out with a golf bag and I try to pretend it's full of snuff films and heroin but I'm starting to cool on you fast. Then I follow you to a Travelodge on the outskirts of town and I think What have we here. The girl you meet in the bar doesn't look like she plays much golf and then you spend two hours and fifteen minutes in room 142 with her and when she comes out and I see the way she's walking and when you leave ten minutes later I recognise that look on your face and I go from cold to boiling again and I raise my glass to you as you walk by me but you're already gone and I have to finish my drink quickly if I'm going to catch up to you.

So I was re-reading what I've written so far back to myself this morning. I wish I had time to go back and change it a bit to make it a bit clearer but what with everything I've been really busy and it feels like I'm running out of time.

Maybe you think that I've made all this stuff up. Ravings of a lunatic et cetera. Maybe you even think you know who I am. I'm an ex-lover of Izzie's, you reckon. Or maybe I'm the same person who sent those weird letters to all your friends, that self-published Harry Potter fanfiction with your name as the author that was basically just Harry sucking off Ron in as many different magical ways possible with the cover of them playing Quidditch not on broomsticks no you guessed it riding big black cocks (I actually didn't write that just downloaded it if you can believe it.) You have a lot of enemies and it's taken all this for you to realise that and now you think you've got it narrowed down to maybe ten or fifteen people and I wonder if your long lost brother you never knew about is on your list just kidding Dexter. But I bet you don't have my face on your imaginary mugshot wall yet so here you are. It's time for the big reveal and you won't need to go ask Tom the barista or your son's football coach or the rental desk at the airport if they remember a guy because you already know me. I mentioned earlier that I gave you a warning and you didn't listen. Now I bet as soon as I tell you this next bit you'll remember. You'll even be able to picture my face and you'll realise you've been wrong this whole time.

You leave the Travelodge in a taxi and you stop off back at the garage and put the golf bag back inside which doesn't have snuff videos or heroin in it but something just as interesting then you go back to the airport and you go to short term parking and get into your own car, the one before you had the 4x4, the Mercedes-Benz. It's silver, of course. I follow you out of the airport and back onto the motorway and I keep repeating the last three letters of your number plate over and over again in my head. INF INF INF. Don't ask me why. I follow you all the way home and by now it's mid-afternoon. It's starting to rain. I wait outside your house for one hour and seven minutes and you come back out again and Izzie is with you. It's the first time I ever see her. She's wearing a green coat. Her hair is scraped back flat against her skull and tied in a ponytail. She looks angry and I'm not surprised you lying liar. You both get into the car and you're heading towards the motorway again, so I overtake you and drive in front of you going way too slowly. I can see in my rear view mirror you're getting angry and Izzie's mouth is still going and going. She's moving her hands about too much and by now it's just starting to get dark it gets dark early at that time of year and it's still raining. Now we're getting close to the roundabout for the motorway and I look back and you're not looking at the road or at me but at Izzie. Your mouth is open in a big O shape and your hand is off the wheel pointing at her. I slam on my

brakes and there's this crunching sound and I feel my balls tingle like I'm in that Ballard book but I don't cum I just put my hazards on and your face is a picture.
I compose myself and get ready for you.
Here I was minding my own business when all of a sudden haha and you get out your wallet and give me £320 and I say That's not enough. Izzie is calling you names so you give me your business card and I say What's this and I rub my neck like it hurts and you say I'll take care of it. I say and here it is this was your first and last warning fairs fair: You should be more careful mister and I take the card and put it in my pocket and you drive off without even saying sorry and you had your chance.
But you didn't listen and so here we are.

So now you know I'm not Izzie's ex-lover (well technically I am three times once in her ass no times with a condom but not the way you were thinking) or a work colleague or an old school friend or your long-lost brother.

I mentioned earlier that I've rented number 63 across the road from your house. That's where I am now, and where I've written most of this. Now because this is a rich person neighbourhood none of the houses are the same inside or out so it isn't like when I was a kid where you go to your friend's house and they just had the furniture in different places but it still felt familiar, the walls were all in the right place, you knew where to find the bog without asking. No, this is going to take some imagination because you've never been inside and I'll have to try to be clear so bear with me here.
Number 63 costs £2,950 a month due on the 20th of every month. I pay by cheque. Upstairs it has four bedrooms and a big bathroom and the middle-sized bedroom is the one with the best view of your house and that's where I am now even though I never open the curtains. Across the landing is the biggest bedroom and that's where I keep most of my work stuff. Clothes my toolkit spares GPS trackers head torch batteries camping gear sleeping bag dried noodles that sort of thing. In the two smallest bedrooms I keep some other stuff I don't want to tell

you about yet. Downstairs it is all modern and open plan like Izzie's office, and the kitchen is sort of against one wall and it has a big breakfast bar/ dining table thing and then a big living area where I have the TV and the sofa and that's where your son spends most of his time since he came to stay with me. There are a couple of French windows that lead out onto a big garden full of trees and there's no neighbours who can see into it so it is pretty secluded and sometimes I leave them unlocked and one time just wide open and your son just carried on playing PlayStation and eating pizza (Meat Feast is his favourite). Now I think that's all the rooms explained except there's a massive garage where I keep two of my vans and there's even a big cellar thing like in the movies which you get down to from the garage and that's where your daughter is. I always keep that door locked. I'm taking no chances with that one. Like I said, she's a real squirmer.

Anyway back to this room again. Have you ever seen *The Lives of Others*? It's German and subtitled so probably not. It's about a Stasi agent who is spying on this political playwright they're not sure they can trust and the agent is listening to every single conversation he's having in his apartment that they've bugged and he's right upstairs in the same building. He sits in a very quiet room at a table with all of his listening equipment around him and he has these headphones on and he has a notebook out and he writes down everything the playwright says that the microphones pick up, and then he goes home and sleeps with fat German prostitutes and sucks on their massive tits and makes himself dinner of rice with tomato ketchup (your son would love that, the rice and ketchup I mean but maybe sucking on the big tits too). Can you picture that in your head? The man at the table listening to everything that happens in the downstairs apartment? OK well that's me. Except I'm across the street not downstairs. And you're obviously the guy he's listening to. Now of course it's not exactly the same. I have much better equipment and I don't just listen I can watch all the camera feeds and I have some other very high tech stuff like infrared and motion sensors and phone intercepts and instead of using a pen and a notebook I'm writing my notes on a laptop but essentially it's the same

thing.
I don't have anything else in here. There are no distractions. When I'm in here I'm either asleep on the camp bed or I'm at the desk here watching you. I even eat here. I suppose these last few days I've been writing this as well which is a bit of a distraction but I'm still watching you except when I'm downstairs with your kids or if I'm out getting things ready for the next part. See for example right now as I'm writing this bit you've been sitting at your dining table and I can see you on two of my monitors one with a good picture of your face and the other you're in profile and you haven't touched your drink in let me check twenty-six minutes and you're staring at nothing just at the wall ahead and there's a bit in *Gone Girl* (the book I haven't seen the movie) where he realises everyone thinks its him because he's behaving so oddly and his twin sister tells him to act normal because he's acting strange enough that people might think he did it and I think that if someone could see you now they'd maybe be thinking about your story a bit more closely because you look like you've won the lottery but the novelty-sized cheque hasn't arrived yet and actually you stole the winning ticket from your senile neighbour that kind of antsy excited. I bet when you read this you'll remember. Now you just downed your whiskey and you're standing up and you go upstairs to your son's room and I think it surprises you that you went there and not to your daughter's room. I think for a minute you're going to do that part in the movie where they fall into the cupboard grabbing all the clothes and rubbing it on their faces for the smell but you don't you just stand there and then go back downstairs and turn on the TV.

I haven't slept in nearly three days so I take five zolpidem and when I wake up I bet my head will be a lot clearer.

Another thing I noticed when I was re-reading this earlier is that I focus on all your bad points too much. Someone who didn't know you reading this will be thinking I know this isn't a nice thing to say and maybe I'm wrong to say it but hear me out what if maybe I'm just saying like what if that guy maybe deserves all this?

I don't think that's really fair do you? It's almost as if this was happening because you were a bad guy with halitosis and a bald patch who everyone at the office despises and we both know it isn't that at all. You're not being punished. I'm not Hannibal Lecter. This isn't happening to you because you're rude or because people who meet you for the first time scrunch up their mouths in a kind of grimace after they've been with you for more than five minutes. There are a lot of people like that, and things like this aren't happening to *them*, are they? I bet some people might even take a dislike to me if they spend long enough with me and the roles were reversed and it was you talking about all the things I did, right?

So here we go. I'm going to balance the scales a bit in your favour. Because you probably need it right now like a morale boost to get you through and I'm in a good mood because the next part is almost ready.

Here are all the good things about you:

I was right. I feel much better. I slept for fifteen hours. I didn't even say anything when I saw the mess your daughter had made. I just hummed some Taylor Swift and cleaned it up.

The name of that girl you met at the Travelodge was M_ K_ but she called herself Katee (don't ask me, that's the way she spelled it) so we'll use that. I always try to be respectful of the dead. You see, originally, I planned to use her in all this, but it didn't really work out like that. Despite the act she used with you the girl was tough. She must have learned judo or kung fu or something before she dropped out of school because she damn near broke my wrist.

I know you really liked her despite the stuff in your golf bag. How do I know that? Because you paid her £2500 a month and most months you only saw her maybe two or three times according to your calendar. I know you had some interesting proclivities but that's about five times more than you really needed to pay to anyone. If there's one thing I've learned about you is that you're tight as a vicar's arse when it comes to money except for things you really care about e.g. holidays cars booze and Katee. Q.E.D.

Like I said before I didn't mean for it to turn out that way and I guess you could say if I had one regret about this then Katee would be it (apart from Izzie of course but that was out of my hands, I have a clear conscience on that one). Not because I liked her particularly and it was pretty obvious that my idea for her wasn't going to work out the minute I saw those muscles, and not even because the way I botched it meant I couldn't even use it in my plan for you. No, I regret it because it is such a fucking cliché. The dead hooker. I mean when all this is said and done I'd prefer no-one ever knew about Katee, least of all you, because it just makes no real sense. She only gets a bit part and to be honest it makes me look bad. Oh look what a surprise he kills hookers you'll say and it makes me seem stupid and if you know I sometimes make mistakes you'll start to think there's another way this ends.

But you see I have this thing about serial killers who kill prostitutes, not because I care particularly about them but it's just so easy and so unoriginal like Come on work a bit for it why don't you? So the only reason I'm mentioning it here is because I feel like I have to justify myself and explain that No, actually, it wasn't like that and I never planned it to work out that way and maybe you'll read it and you won't have the reaction I was hoping for but I guess that's just another dilemma because I feel like if I don't put it down here now it'll bug me for ages and I just can't tell Chloe about it and like that BT ad used to say Its Good To Talk.

I feel like I don't have to leave stuff out like the other stories because back then I saw it all happening very differently to the way it actually did. So here you go a little insight into the draft version behind the curtain, a real glimpse of Oz.

Katee arrives at my hotel room at about midnight. She has sleek brown hair like it's made of something other than hair, if you know what I mean, and I immediately want to touch it but obviously I can't yet because I haven't shown her the money as Jerry Maguire would say. She walks past me and I smell her perfume and I feel my dick crawling up my thigh already and I

look at her back and I see right away two things:
That she's worth every penny you pay her
That my original plan for her is 100% going to fail
The hooker that turns her back on you inside five seconds is not the kind of hooker you can mess around with but I'm feeling cocky and horny and I think what the hell. After all I managed to find her within three days of our fender-bender and I must admit it was some pretty good detective work. But when I see the way she moves across the room I know the original plan won't work and so I think on my feet and try another angle.
Before we get to that part though I can't resist so we joke around a couple of times and that's always a mistake. Afterwards as she's getting out of the shower she catches me looking at the marks on her body that you'd only notice in a bathroom light where there's no shadow and the makeup has washed off. I didn't plan it but it was obvious she saw me looking so I said I hope you made that bastard pay and she ignores me and I said You know there are other ways you can take his money and she speaks for the first time and I realise that she's Scottish Edinburgh I think. Oh yeah? she says, just that. Cool, like something out of a noir movie. So I explain to her about what you could do with some well placed cameras et cetera and she just stares at me and I know I've blown it and she won't come back again she's thinking cops or worse and I shouldn't have slept with her because I can't fucking think straight and she's getting dressed and I see her getting away from me but I breathe through my nose a few times and she picks up my wallet and takes another £200 and she leaves without saying anything else just that first Oh yeah?

My favourite short story isn't Choke but let's pretend it is. Here's the basic rundown so you don't have to waste time looking it up.
A boy hears this story about a great way to get off (there's other ways mentioned but this is the best). So what you do is you swim down to the bottom of your pool and sit on the little filter pump thing and it sucks at your ass and if you do it just right it gives you the biggest ejaculation you've ever had. Something to do with the prostate. This is America by the way, where they all

have their own pools; you can't go and do this at the leisure centre. So anyway this kid thinks Fuck yeah that sounds plausible and not at all dangerous let's try this so he does. Only when he gets to the bottom of the pool and pulls down his trunks and sits on the filter bit he knows straight away that something's wrong. He feels it tugging at his ass all right but there's too much sucking. Oh god no my ass has formed a tight seal around the filter and Oh god I can feel my insides moving inside me and Oh right I'm stuck underwater and I can't breathe I think I'm going to drown and my guts are being sucked out through my asshole.

And it's that moment. Oh that moment. That clear crystal diamond bullet that drives its way through the front of your skull. That moment when you know, without a single shred of doubt, that you are *fucked*. You feel the panic, feel the reptile taking over, that puckering asshole, that lurch of the stomach, that hot fire in your thighs, the stars dancing across your eyeballs. That moment when the handle of your mom's toothbrush slips through your vaselineshit fingers up into your ass. That moment when you're surfing and you feel something brush against your board. That moment when you're pumping the brakes and flashing your lights but the jackknifing lorry just isn't turning. That moment when you're half way through falling and you can see the ground rushing up at your face and your arms aren't working. That moment when the guy you're hitting has five friends you didn't see. That moment when you hear the pilot yelling from the cockpit and the oxygen masks drop. That moment when you pull the ripcord of the reserve parachute and it comes away in your hands. That moment when three white pickups pull your tour group over in the desert. That moment when you feel a shove in your back and you're falling off the platform and you hear the squeal of brakes. That moment when a serial killer has stolen your kids but you can't tell the cops because you killed your wife and everyone thinks she ran away with them to Spain.

The kid has to chew through his unspooled intestines to get himself free. I don't remember if he lives or not but that's not the point. It doesn't really matter. In that moment, he knows he's absolutely fucked. He does the only thing he can do. He lets the reptile take over. You'd do the same. So would I. He tears at his guts with his teeth as they're unravelling from his ass. He's like a fucking fish on a hook thrashing about because that's what makes us animals and you still don't understand yet but you will.

I find a bit of ham sandwich floating in the makeshift cellar toilet today and that explains a lot. Everyone gets cranky when they're hungry. I go back upstairs and say to your son Just popping out I'll be back in twenty minutes and he says Fine. I drive to Tesco and pick up a few things and come back after about twenty minutes and it doesn't look like he's moved and I say Do you want some lunch and he says Sure so I take out the steaks and he watches me cook them and I take one of the steaks off the grill after about a minute and put it on a plate and he asks Who's that for? and I don't answer and we eat the other two steaks but he keeps looking at the other one on the side. While he eats ice cream I go upstairs and get a DVD and then take the blue steak into the garage and down the stairs to the cellar. I put the DVD in and place the steak in front of your daughter and say Eat it and then press play and the PETA video starts and she just looks at me. Then I go back upstairs and come back down again after about seventy minutes and she hasn't eaten it so I take it away and I go back upstairs and got another DVD and go back downstairs and take out the PETA one and put the other one in. You might have seen it. *Marathon Man*. Then I go over to the tool rack and take down a claw hammer and put it on the table next to me and sit and watch *Marathon Man* with her and skip to the good parts. When the credits start I look at her and then I go upstairs and make dinner. We have pork chops. I eat with your son who tells me about a new game that has just come out on PlayStation and I tell him he can download it and he looks so happy. He's forgotten that third steak already. Then I go upstairs and watch you for a bit while I download another film because I don't have it on DVD. When it's done I burn it to a DVD and go and fetch the leftover pork chops and take them into the cellar and we sit and watch *Babe* together while she eats the cold pork chops and after she's done and has stopped crying I say That'll do pig and I laugh.

Now when was the last time you spent that much time alone with your daughter? (Don't tell me I know).

Pornhub lies to you. Those hot Californians sitting with their legs crossed on that black sofa chewing gum in their tight t-shirts and high heels answering those questions so everyone knows they're there to be gangbanged for three hours by four men with abnormally large cocks because they want to be (haha)? That's not real life. They don't just undress and suddenly you have your cock in their ass. Seriously don't even try that. They edit all the boring stuff out remember. You have to get them to shave first otherwise they have these little pubey hairs around their ass. And you can't just use a bit of spit to clean it I mean you have to get them to scrub right up in there or you'll get streaks of shit all over your dick. And you have to use lube. I know it doesn't look like they do on Pornhub but seriously you have to because otherwise it isn't fun for either of you. After all she's doing you a big favour. Is a bit of lube really that much to ask?
I'm pleased to say Izzie had shaved those gross little hairs and cleaned right up in there and brought plenty of lube. I guess she'd done it a few times before.

I run down the stairs of the Travelodge and catch up with Katee just as she's getting into her car, a BMW X3, black, brand new maybe two or three months old if that. She hears my footsteps and she turns around to face me, cool as a fucking cat, her hand already inside her bag for the pepper spray. She doesn't take it out. She just raises an eyebrow at me and says Yeah?
I try to explain. I can't remember what I said. I can tell she really isn't interested. I've totally misread the situation. You're one of her easier clients, and even if she were the type to kiss and plant a spycam and blackmail the shit out of you there are plenty of better marks than the guy with the golf bag. I realise that maybe some of the bruises aren't even yours and as we're standing out in that carpark I suddenly get very conscious of the cameras and I feel like I'm being trapped, feel like a fucking idiot for thinking I could use her in any of my plans. I start to back off, and she just gets into the BMW and drives off without looking back at me.

See? I told you. Telling you that makes me look bad, makes me look like I'm not in control, and like I said before, I really can't have that. Just remember that I'm only telling you this to hurt you more later, OK?

Another thing I enjoy doing in my spare time is watching jihadi videos. You know the ones I mean, where they have the white guy in the orange jumpsuit on his knees and scrolling Arabic covers half the screen. I can't get enough of them. Now I know what you're thinking. But I don't watch them for the gore. No, honestly. I watch it because I can't get over how seriously these young men take themselves. I mean the whole world is watching and they're so po-faced about it all. Why not have a little fun with your captive audience? (Ha.) They have millions of people watching and I bet some pretty important people too, like the Pentagon and all those other old cunts who have to watch and analyse as they're chewing on their cigars. So why stick to the same old script?

If it were me I'd maybe get our biggest baddest recruit and get them to fight the scrawny white guy to the death ARE YOU NOT ENTERTAINED or round a few up and have them battle it out TWO MEN ENTER ONE MAN LEAVES or let them loose in the mountains and chase them down like *Running Man* or Robert Hansen. A bit of a spectacle, you know? Once you've seen one beheading and all that. You still get to kill them and you can still put the bits in about the caliphate and Saudi bases yadda yadda. Maybe even more people would watch if you showed a bit of a lighter side. I also like when the guys who are about to get their heads hacked off convert to Islam and grow out their beards. That cracks me up. Or pleading for Muhammed Al-Ackbar or some other war criminal to be released from a Jordanian prison. They can feel the pool filter's grasp on their insides and they're chewing and chewing and chewing and they don't know they're already dead. Like that's going to stop them you stupid fucking cunt don't you understand THIS DOESN'T END WELL FOR YOU I feel like saying to them.

Three days after I blew it with Katee I got an email from Chloe asking me to come give her a hand with some business. The way things had gone I wasn't exactly hopeful that my plan for you would work anymore so I jumped at the chance.

I arrive in Florence really early in the morning. Chloe meets me at a cafe and explains the situation and I say This sounds like fun and take a sip of my espresso and she smiles but I can see she's actually a bit stressed because the guy has hired some serious people and everyone else we work with is tied up with other jobs so it's down to us.

The killing is just a perk of the day job, really. You'd be surprised how infrequently I get to exercise those particular muscles in my profession, especially at the level we're at now. We tend to outsource the rough work, and when you're dealing with marks in the circles we do there's just so little need for it outside of the occasional act of self-preservation.

Having said that there are still times when having someone like me available really does come in handy. I have a propensity for violence that someone being paid to clear up a mess just doesn't have. And why would they? They're really only interesting in the bottom line. To them, everything is a strict risk calculation. That's why so many of them work in pairs. They favour the drive-by or the car bomb or the poisoned martini or the sniper rifle. They're reluctant to get too close. They always want to have one foot on the pedal if it looks like going pear-shaped (which reminds me, that's another great torture method: they stuff a pear-shaped device up the guy's asshole and there's a screw you can turn that slowly opens out the sides. It's called the Pear of Anguish - go look it up. I even stole a real one a few years ago from a museum but I left it at an old safehouse and never got around to going back for the thing.)

So anyway as you've probably guessed the plan involved a spot of violence, and as no-one else is available and I don't really mind a bit of risk, as you'll probably have already worked out, it's down to me to sort it all out.

The misbehaving mark is a wealthy guy named Valentino P__. His parents are rich, real estate and fashion. Valentino has a young wife, two small daughters, and a large entourage. Unusually for someone so loaded, he almost never leaves Italy, maybe once or twice a year and only then to visit New York or Tokyo for a few days in his private jet. He spends most of his life in his large compound, at the beach, or in one of the small restaurants in the hills around N_. He rarely visits friends (they prefer to take advantage of his hospitality) and always travels with a retinue of bodyguards. He boasts of connections to the South but neither Chloe nor I could find any evidence of that, and if he did it was tenuous enough for us not to worry.

We are taking him for a fairly minor €10k a month for some indiscretions with five Nigerian twelve-year old prostitutes (for the colour of their skin as much as for their age). No need for Photoshop on this one. Why so little, you ask? Well the pictures were infrared green and certainly contestable, and the Nigerians had up and disappeared as soon as we put in the first claim. It was a minor project, one we both knew would probably fizzle out after a year or so. Neither of us was too bothered about managing the claims. We were happy to ride it for the course before letting it wither on the vine. No great gain, no great loss. Just business as usual.

Then Chloe gets wind that someone is looking closely at the Nigerians, and specifically the contact we acquired the pictures from. Then our source ends up dead, mutilated, the whereabouts of his head unknown, and Chloe is seeing Valentino move lots of money around.

She gets the hint. I leave on the next flight out.

At first we're both thinking the same thing. Release the pictures and get the fuck out of town. Maybe try and steal some cash from the accounts we'd got our hands on to cover our exit fees. But a mark killing our source sends a bad message. There's just no way we can do the legwork on all these projects these days, and we rely on contractors more than you'd think. And if the guys sitting out in the rain with their video cameras and drones and telephoto lenses and spyware hear our sources are getting knocked off without consequences? Well, you're a business strategist, aren't you? That's just poor relationship management.

Chloe is thinking the two little girls but I know that Valentino will have his best men with them. Then we're thinking the mistresses, but they're so transitory that it'd be of little value.

The wife is a possibility, and I keep that in mind in case nothing else comes up.

A few days of digging around later, something does.

It turns out Valentino has a younger brother, Paolo. Paolo is very different to Valentino and his parents. He is not in the business. He dropped out of the expensive foreign university his parents sent him to at nineteen, refused a position in the family firm, sent back the trust cheques by return mail, and now lives three hundred kilometres to the north on a small remote farm with his wife and young son. They are poor. They don't have a car, just a ten year old motorbike. They drink rough wine and eat black bread. They are good, hard-working people. They dote on their son, and they sit around the table at night next to a small gaslight, helping him with his school work and listening to his stories about his friends. All very rustic and quaint and nineteenth century, like something out of a picture.

Paolo, his wife, and his child are entirely innocent of the sins of his brother and their family. As far as I can tell, he is a good, loyal husband, and an excellent role model and father to his child. In fact he's so innocent, so unconnected, and most of all so *poor* that neither Valentino nor anyone in his entourage or security firm ever consider that someone wanting to fuck with him might drive the three hundred kilometres up the winding roads to rural G__, wait until Paolo leaves on the bike to travel down to the town, and maybe teach Valentino a little lesson vicariously. It doesn't cross their minds once. He's a nobody, he's an innocent, he's a pure soul, what has Paolo ever done to anybody?

I was inspired by that scene in Gladiator. You remember it? Poor old Maximus is on his horse, looking more than a little peaky. He's just escaped, and he's riding back to the family farm as fast as he can. Meanwhile over at the farm wifey and sonny are taunting a pony when, uh oh, some guys on horses are riding ominously down the avenue toward them. Back over on his horse Maximus sees a vision of this and he miraculously recovers and kicks his horse and the music picks up and the horse starts galloping. Over at the farm sonny has run down the road towards the bad guys on horses and wifey's screaming at him but he just stands there like a deaf mute and I run him down in my Alfa Romeo 4C, shoot wifey in the face, string them both up over a tree in the garden and burn the miserable fucking hovel to the ground. I'm gone before Paolo sees the smoke drifting over the hills toward the town.

Now you're asking yourself Why the hell is he telling me this? Does he get a kick out of it? Does he enjoy making me listen to his stories about killing women and children, knowing that he's got my kids? Well yes, of course, all of the above. But I'm also telling you this for a couple of other reasons:

One, to explain why it ended up like that with Katee. I had other business to attend to. If I hadn't have been distracted it might have ended up differently with her.

And two, and more importantly, I'm telling you this so you'll realise that I have absolutely no problem about killing innocents. I've done it plenty of times before. I don't care what kind of people your kids are. I don't care if they're golden and brilliant or the next Einstein or, conversely, the next Genghis Khan. They are interesting to me only insomuch as they are interesting to you, and I will not hesitate to cut them into a thousand little pieces in front of one another if you do not act precisely as I want you to.

American Psycho does pop music and *Cable Guy* does movies and *Hannibal* does classical music and art and I guess that leaves me with either games or ancient history but you won't get any of the fucking references you fucking ignoramus and for some reason that bothers me I had a whole list of really good Iago quotes (*Othello* not *Aladdin*, dickhead) ready but what's the point. And if you didn't get it before your daughter thought I was going to pull out her teeth if she didn't eat the bloody steak I shouldn't have to explain this but sometimes I think if I don't you'll miss it.

So you probably stopped reading back when I mentioned the garage. In fact I bet you a million pounds you did. Because if I know where the garage is I might have been there, say, three days ago.

Well welcome back anyway. Whiskey is good for shock. Her suitcase is at my cottage. So are your clothes and your golf bag and the rest of your stuff. You should have burned it all. And now you're thinking Oh god Oh god and then you leave again and when you get to number 63 and you break in through the French windows around the back and you realise its exactly the way I described it and you find the claw hammer I left for you in the cellar you start to really panic maybe even do a little dry heave or maybe a real one and now maybe you'll fucking sit down and finish reading this OK?

I get back from Italy and I'm feeling good again. Refreshed. The first thing I do is drive to your house. I've only seen you in person four times but they're all so vivid in my memory. Airplane Travelodge Fender Bender Pizza Express. Like I can't stop thinking about them. I guess I'd kind of put Katee out of my mind. And then I see Izzie again and the kids coming out of the house and this'll sound strange but it was like they were my family, you know? Haha just joking but I admit I'd forgotten how good Izzie looked she was wearing this really nice long dress and you could see the freckles across her chest and her shoulders were shiny like she's just moisturised and I could imagine exactly how they smelled and even though yes she was a bit heavy around the middle it was the right kind of heavy. I sat there and thought of the way it'd look when she bent over and she gets closer and closer and my mouth just opens and she sits down into it pressing her cunt into my face and rubbing her clit along my bottom teeth and then she takes my cock and puts it all the way into her mouth until I can hear her gagging on it and she laughs a bit and sits down harder on me now and she's got her full weight on me and I close my eyes and all I can smell is her asshole and it smells like aloe vera and warm skin.

So it's maybe a week after I flew back from Florence and saw Izzie again at your house and I get another email from Chloe. It isn't anything important, but for some reason it reminds me of Katee and that stupid night and I realise that there's just a chance that she might say something to you. Maybe I'm being paranoid, but who knows. I didn't really know what kind of relationship you two had and now I'd decided to go ahead, I

realised it was time to get serious. I got out my list, and at the top I added:
Sort out Katee

I keep talking about Chloe. Chloe this Chloe that. I bet you're getting sick of having to read it all right? Or maybe you're cleverer than I give you credit for (you're not; it should be pretty fucking obvious by now). Maybe you've realised Wait a minute why am I hearing so much about this Chloe? What's so important about this person? And now you're starting to get really scared, and if you weren't before maybe you are now, maybe you're putting the pieces together. Because if she is who you think she is then it really is all over. Your guts feel like they're getting sucked down the drain and you're done, your last get out of jail free card cut up into a million little pieces.
Yes, you've guessed it. Chloe is Josie. Yes, *that* Josie. Your Josie.

The CIA play recordings of screaming women to terrorists to make them talk. They say We have your wife Muhammed. Can't you hear her next door? You better spill the beans now or else. That always seemed so stupid. Any good terrorist worth his weight in semtex would know what his wife's screams sounded like.

You fly to the continent for work about once every couple of weeks which gives you plenty of time to joke around with Josie and me plenty of time to spend watching Izzie and the kids. Sometimes I come with you on your business trips but it's harder for me to keep tabs on you at all those different hotels and convention centres and meeting rooms and since you see Chloe I mean Josie it doesn't really make a difference as I hear about it all anyway.
So here's a typical day when you're off out of the country working hard talking bullshit to rich morons about innovation and creativity and diffusion and synergy and convergence:
I follow Izzie everywhere she goes.
I dream about the ways I'm going to make you bite down on your pillow at night.

I plan ways to make your family hate you more than they already do.

I go into your house at four in the morning and sit at your dining table in the dark and think things like If anyone comes downstairs in the next hour I'll slit their throat and make blood pudding.

I try to work out how long I could keep Izzie alive with a cactus in her uterus.

I imagine your plane crashing on your way back and wonder how long your family would mourn you (however long the insurance paperwork took to file, I reckon). Then I try to figure out how long before I could move in with Izzie and replace you.

I rub your toothbrush on things.

I very carefully remove pages from your GQ with a razor blade.

I wonder what your son's lungs will taste like (with a big Amarone, ha).

I break into your office in the middle of the night and sit at your chair and bash on the keyboard and pick up the phone and pretend I'm you and laugh at my own jokes.

I picture your face when you finally realise everything.

I log onto your computer and clear your saved passwords.

I creep into your daughter's room and imagine all kinds of things.

So even though I quite like when you're away I prefer it when you're back home because when I'm bored my mind tends to run away with itself and I spend too much time being reckless and/or daydreaming.

I'm there in the coffee shop when you get the text off Katee. I can't see your face from where I'm sitting but your shoulders tense up so I know you've read it. Katee never sent it, of course. I did. You get up. I follow you out into the street. It's sunny so I put on my sunglasses and can smell the dog shit baking on the tarmac and the fag ends and the exhaust fumes and it makes me feel good to be alive. Poor Katee. You walk around for a bit obviously not going anywhere because you walk past the coffee place twice. Then you go into the multi-storey and get into your car but you forget to pay at the machine. You get to the barrier

and it's only then you realise and there's a long line behind you already and you have to press the button and I can hear you shouting even through my helmet. Eventually everyone backs up and I see your face for the first time as you drive by.
How does it make you feel that I can make your face look like that by sending you a three sentence text? I spent maybe five minutes coming up with it and I bet you still remember what it said, don't you? That's a pretty impressive work:result ratio. Your colleagues would give me a high score on their evaluation tests for that kind of thing I bet.

I hacked your Skype so that sometimes in video conferences even though it shows your microphone is muted and your camera is off they really aren't. You shouldn't pick your nose so much.

In *The Music of Chance* by Paul Auster a down on his luck guy named Nashe meets this cocky young kid, Jack Pozzi, who's this hotshot poker player. This Pozzi kid knows about this big high stakes card game that a couple of gay eccentric millionaires are hosting, only he hasn't got the dosh to get in. Pozzi persuades Nashe to lend him the entry fee. So far, so Elmore Leonard. But it all goes wrong. The kid is too reckless, or the game is fixed, or Pozzi just isn't as great as he thinks. The millionaires wipe the floor with young Pozzi, and after some pretty bad decisions and some increasingly stupid bets, both Pozzi and Nashe end up having to work off their gambling debt by building this big fuck off wall to nowhere on the millionaires' estate.
It's hard work. The kid Pozzi doesn't take to it well. After no time at all he's running up even more debts to the queers by calling in hookers and getting shitfaced in the caravan he shares with Nashe as they work on the wall. He's got all this energy bottled up and this new life, however short-term, is killing him. He can't face it, can't see beyond the next stone, can't see anything but what he's missing out on. How he can't do anything he used to enjoy doing, how his whole life revolves around building a boring ass wall day after day after day.
Nashe, on the other hand, he doesn't particularly like the way

things have turned out, but he seems to see it for what it is. Hard work, sure, but what other choice is there? He plays the hand he's been given. He gets up in the morning and does his day's work, laying down stone after stone. He tries to explain to the kid why it has to be like this, but he can't get through to Pozzi. They just look at the thing so differently, you know?

Eventually Nashe even comes to enjoy the work. Feeling the ache in his back and seeing that long wall that he's made with his own sweat from just those small little actions it takes to get that stone into place is surprisingly satisfying. When he looks back at what he's built so far he can't help feeling a little proud, and maybe he even looks ahead to where he knows he's going to put down more stones tomorrow and the next day and he feels maybe a little bit of anticipation. Maybe that's what Mr Twit felt like sticking on all those slivers of wood. Nashe feels like now his life actually means something, feels like he's got a purpose again. A reason to get up in the morning, a reason to keep sucking down air. The wall means something to him, however pointless it seems to Pozzi or anyone else. The wall is *important*.

Now sometimes I'm like Pozzi. I have my moments. Fuck the wall, fuck these stones, I want to see some fucking progress and when I don't, when I only put down two or three stones and my back is fucking breaking and I stink and my head pounds, I want to give it all up. I want to go out and blow everything on vodka and cocaine and hookers and fly a fucking airplane into a fucking skyscraper and throw napalm at nuns or drive a tank down the fucking motorway and strap an atom bomb to my chest and fuck that fucking wall and those little fucking stones fuck all of it.

But mostly I'm Nashe. Mostly I get up and go to my wall to nowhere and I place that one stone down, then another, then another, because what else is there to do? What else do I have but this fucking wall?

3.

You wear badly fitting shirts and you click your teeth against your fork every single fucking meal. You wear too much aftershave and you always miss three hairs underneath your left nostril when you shave. Oh and read a book every now and again you fucking moron. No the newspaper doesn't count.

The Agency keeps sending me everyone on their books but her. There's a cross and her name next to my mobile number in their database (They might be Elite but they're not Discreet. They keep their client list unencrypted it was in a fucking .csv file if you can believe that). It takes me a few days to work out where she lives. She has an apartment on S__ Road which is no good to me at all because I know that area and I know the kind of place she must have and there's no way I can do it there. The walls are too thin and the neighbours are nosey and the windows are floor to ceiling and the stairwell is well-lit and the car park has CCTV. That neighbourhood has terrible parking, permit only, so I couldn't even stake it out and follow her to the shops or anything. I spend all afternoon racking my brain, wondering how often she had to show at the Agency office, figuring out the best places to wait for her there, whether to take the van or rent an estate. Then I think maybe I should hack her email and her calendar and follow her to a client but that's hard and the Agency only has her mobile number for her and without being close to her for longer than two minutes it's going to be tricky to break into and by then she's bound to recognise me. Then I think I should switch phones and try the Agency again and hope I get lucky and they send her first but I know despite their poor computer security they're otherwise very careful and I don't have any reference except for you and they make new clients do an interview first (We Come To You For A Discreet Discussion of Your Desires) so they know your face in case of crazies and they're bound to be suspicious even if I could fake it and if they

don't send her first the other girls will probably recognise me and then that's it.
Pretty stupid huh? It wasn't until my fifth or sixth coffee that I finally figured it out, and only then because I opened the feed on my tablet to watch you at work (it helps distract me). I knew exactly where she'd be maybe once or twice a month. I just had to wait until you got horny again.

I remember a funny story I read in a local paper when I lived in Europe a few years ago. I was trying to brush up on my language skills, so every morning I'd head to the local cafe, pick up a paper, open up the translate function on my phone and slog through the thing.
It was a small town. There was some trouble with connected Ukrainians from a recent job, and Chloe and I decided lying low for a few months in a tiny Alpine town might not be a bad idea. So the local newspaper I practiced on every morning was filled with stories about potholes and fundraisers and that kind of thing. Small town news. Then one morning, sipping on my espresso, smoking cigarettes that still tasted foreign after eight years, frowning over the newspaper line by line, I read a great little story. A real cracker. It can only have been a few lines, shorter than the time I've just spent introducing it. An unnamed local man found cookies laced with rat poison on a bench in the local playground.
Now I know what you're thinking. The sick bastard is laughing at the idea of sweet little Klaus and Claudette eating those poisoned cookies and throwing up their guts right there all over that playground. But that's not it. (And no, I didn't have anything to do with it. I have better things to do with my time). You've got me all wrong. No, I'm far more interested by the local man in the story. I spent the rest of the day thinking about local man.
I could picture maybe one of two things happening.
Local man finds some discarded cookies left in a playground, like he said. But then, instead of throwing them away, local man figures that the only possible reason someone has left cookies in a playground is for nefarious purposes and they must be suspicious, probably poisoned. Local man takes the box of

cookies to the local police, who actually listen to his crazy theory. They find it totally plausible and think What a great way to spend taxpayers' money testing garbage people bring us off the street, and they pay actual real money to have the cookies sent off by express mail to a forensic laboratory for testing by people with doctorates, AND PARANOID LOCAL MAN WAS PROVED RIGHT.

I guess that could have happened, but here's my personal theory. Local man was the one who laced the cookies with rat poison. Someone sees him leave the cookies and politely reminds him about littering. He lies, and claims he just found the cookies there. But then he panics. He's new to this. We've all been there. He goes overboard, starts talking too much to cover up his mistake. He says They're not mine but hey do you reckon they might be poisoned or something maybe I should take them to the police station for checking up on you can never be too careful in this idyllic Alpine town we live in in which nothing has or ever will happen. The local police listen to local man's story, take one long look up and down at him, realise they can't prove it was local man that laced the cookies with rat poison but test the things anyway and make it pretty obvious that they know it was him and local man gets the message loud and clear and he realises he'll have to be much more careful and maybe drive to the next Alpine town next time around.

It was a few hours later before I realised there was another way it could have played out. Maybe it's the obvious one, I don't know.

Local man sees the cookies left out by another local man who's fed up with all the rats in his garden. Local man feels a bit peckish, and takes a bite. They taste funny so he chucks them in the bin and when he becomes unwell a few hours later he remembers the funny tasting cookies, goes back to the bin, and takes the remains to the police station and tells them the story.

Perhaps that's the way everyone else who read it saw it playing out. I don't know. But that one story made me realise for the first time in ages how differently I see the world to everyone else. It's like *Life of Pi*. I much prefer the version without the tiger, and I still like to think local man was a bungling child poisoner.

I walk across the lawn like a mouse. I see your sister-in-law inside on the phone, and it makes me a little sad that you won't get to see that call on your bill and make that pouty-angry face like you always do. I know your daughter is upstairs in her bedroom and as I cross the garden I can hear music drifting out of her window.

One thing you should know about me is that sometimes, however much I think about the way I'm going to do something, when it actually comes to doing the thing I suddenly get another idea. Usually it's a fucking stupid one, but it seems clever or funny to me at the time. And once I have that idea I can't shake it. I just can't help myself. I have to do it. It's like Tourette's or something, the Pozzi in me coming out. Case in point: I knew I had to get rid of Harriet. I spent fifteen days waiting for the right moment when I could pull it off. But of course when I get to the house I couldn't just leave the door open and wait until Harriet came out like I'd planned. I got that stupid Humans Can Lick Too idea in my head, and once it was in there I couldn't get it out, even though when I think back it was a fucking stupid idea and risky as hell and so many things could have gone wrong. But that's how my brain works sometimes.

And other times I stick to my plan to the letter. I'm Nashe. I steal your daughter without harming a hair on her head. Just another brick in the wall.

It's your anniversary and for once I'm actually impressed. You have tickets for the Itzhak Perlman recital and a table booked at Y_ afterwards. You're wearing a clean white shirt and a smart black tie and Izzie is wearing an evening gown and you are opening doors and smiling at her and the taxi arrived on time and the babysitter is watching TV with the kids and everything is going well, exactly as you planned, and I start to feel a bit bad for Izzie. Classical music makes me grind my teeth so I wait in the lobby for you and at the interval you drink champagne and for once don't make a comment about its nose and you eat £8 ice cream and then you go back in when the bell sounds and somehow you're both still having a good time as if you've forgotten how you normally behave and meeting Josie has really worked wonders on you it's like you're a new man, Katee who?

The table at the restaurant is a good one and you order for Izzie in French and she runs her fingers over her left cheek like she does when she's happy. I couldn't get a table for one but it doesn't matter I can watch from outside in my van and the microphone on your phone is picking up everything really clearly so I can hear every word you are saying anyway. You clink glasses even though you normally hate that and Izzie's smile gets bigger and you make small talk for a bit then Izzie excuses herself and you even watch her go as she walks to the bathroom.

I press send on the WhatsApp message after she's been gone two minutes. Your phone buzzes and I take my headphones off as you reach into your breast pocket for your phone. I fetch out my binoculars and focus in on your face as you unlock your phone 1379.

What's this I see you thinking Why is Izzie messaging me from the bathroom? and then you open it and it says Hi hun miss u like crazy can't wait to see u tomorrow I have big surprise for u I'll be wearing ur favourite xxx and your face, your face, your face and you gulp your wine and I can see you looking around and you have to eat something you feel sick so you stuff the posh bread in your mouth and then Izzie is coming back and you're pale and I've judged it perfectly because you don't say a word you just look at her and try this weak smile and Izzie smiles back this big toothy smile and I put my headphones back on and I hear her say I can't wait to try the lamb and you just say Yes and the conversation stops and then the waiter comes over with the hors-d'oeuvre and you're trying your best to eat but Izzie might be a bit drunk but she's not stupid and she says You ok? and you just mumble Yes fine and it goes on like that for a while and Izzie's not rubbing her cheek anymore they're flushed because she's drinking too much because you're not saying anything and to be honest you look like you're about to throw up everywhere.

Eventually she gets bored and she pulls out her phone and I see you watching her like a hawk you're expecting her to look up in shock when she realises she's sent the message to you by accident but of course she doesn't because she didn't send the message I did and when she puts the phone away you're scowling and the waiter finally comes over with the bill to put you both out of your misery and as you're punching in your pin number you try your best to be casual and say So any plans for tomorrow? and I actually laugh out loud in my van and Izzie shrugs and says Oh nothing much I thought I'd drive up and see Mum and you raise an eyebrow and she says Did you want to come? and she pulls a face because she really is going to see her parents she only jokes around when you're on your business trips and the thought of you coming along doesn't exactly fill her with excitement because whenever you go to their house you act like a tosser and keep talking about doing up the kitchen and nosing around like an estate agent and you're so fucking obvious but you see the look she pulls and misunderstand and you kind of croak and say Oh no I have plans too and by then I'm laughing so hard I drop the binoculars on the floor and they crack and they were really expensive but it's absolutely worth it to see that look on your face.

I'm probably watching you read this by the way. You won't find all the cameras.

Katee knows straight away how much trouble she's in. Before I can get her inside the van she kicks out and catches me in the balls and I have to hit her really hard in the back of the head with the jack to get a bit of breathing room.
I hit her again even though she's on the floor of the van. It's a good job I do because she was just pretending to be out and she grabs my wrist and I think Fuck she's quick and her foot's in my stomach and before I know it she's thrown me right over her into the van like she's a fucking trebuchet and I lose hold of the jack and have to scramble to the door and catch her by the hair just as she's about to slam it on me and I manage to pull her in and she yells and I feel a big chunk of her hair tear right out of her scalp and then she's trying to do another one of her fucking kung fu moves on me but this time I see it coming because the second hit with the jack knocked her half senseless and even

though my wrist is on fire I kind of deflect her arm trying to grab me and get her head in a lock and I slam her face into the side of the van and I hear a crunch and she's out this time properly her legs go limp. Wax on wax off bitch I say like a fucking movie villain and I laugh but it's more of a cough and I close the van door.

I had to wear a sling for a week and it was all I could do to go hire a VW beetle and hang around the university and introduce myself to girls wearing jeans Hi I'm Ted I'm having a little trouble getting my bag to the car could you please haha but seriously that fucking bitch really fucked up my wrist and I admit I may have taken it out on her a little bit. I'm not usually easily upset but when I do lose it I go apeshit. It took me nearly an hour to remove all the incriminating evidence and in the end I just said Fuck it and burned her and the van in the woods.

Even though I covered it up the private detective the Agency contracted followed you for three weeks. It wasn't until they pulled the security tape from the P_ Hotel bar and saw you waiting around like Billy No Mates for three hours with your golf bag and that combined with the fake withdrawals on her bank account in Moscow and they realised you probably weren't involved. They had a lot of shady Russians in their unencrypted database and some of them preferred having their princesses locked up in their dacha just for themselves and E&D just put it down as the cost of doing business like anything else Sometimes these things happen what are you going to do you can't save all of them.

A fortnight after your anniversary you torrent three adult films (without using a VPN. Idiot). You have the house to yourself for the weekend. Izzie has taken the kids to their grandparents'. The sun is shining. You spend most of Saturday afternoon playing golf with James and Graham before heading to the clubhouse for drinks. You guzzle four glasses of Dalwhinnie in under an hour and dominate the conversation. James and Graham leave early. You drink another two glasses of Dalwhinnie and spend twelve minutes leering at Milena, a waitress with dark brown hair and absolutely zero interest in you. You pay the bill and leave. You drive home because you're irresponsible. You nearly crash the car twice. You arrive home just after six. You go down to the cellar and pick out a 2005 Bordeaux. You order a Domino's pizza, which will go well with your £250 wine. You drink two pilsners while you wait for the wine to breathe and the pizza to arrive, which, remarkably, coincide.

At seven thirty I text Hannah, the babysitter who lives two streets over, asking her to come and look after the children between eight and eleven thirty, £40, Our taxi jst arrived so let urself in c u later. She immediately agrees NP hf x. I change the message sender from Izzie to Mrs R_ a couple of minutes later in case someone ever checks. Meanwhile, you turn on your computer and switch on the TV and select HDMI 2 with the remote. I open the door of the van and hop out into the warm evening air and jog to the front of the house and unlock the door and leave it on the latch. When I get back to the van you have opened the first of the torrented adult films and begun your third slice of pizza. You skip the first two minutes and turn up the volume. The lady in the movie is already naked and strapped to a device that simulates sexual intercourse with a rapacious and anatomically disproportionate machine. A large dildo attached to a mechanical arm that rotates like a catherine wheel is penetrating her vagina at around two hundred thrusts a minute, and she is not enjoying it. A man's hairy hand appears occasionally brandishing a whip, which he hits her with. She cries out even though there is a bright pink ball gag in her mouth. The cry has a distinctly wet sound. Dark, raised lines have begun to appear on her breasts and stomach where the man has hit her. Her name is Starla. She lives in Los Angeles California but she was born in Broomfield Colorado. She is on Twitter @starlaTV. She is thirty four years old and too old and too tall and her breasts are starting to get that wrinkled deflating balloon look underneath where the skin is separating from the implants. She doesn't get much work except for these kinds of videos now. You are not following her on Twitter, and do not know her name or that she lives in Los Angeles California or her work situation, but you are touching your penis with a greasy pizza hand anyway. You are very drunk and I am recording this.

You roll down your trousers so as so to get better access to your asshole, which you are attempting to stick two fingers into without proper lubrication. You are very drunk. You have slipped down the sofa and are making little grunting noises as you rub your smaller than average penis.

Unfortunately, Hannah walks up the drive ten minutes early. I scold her for this, but she doesn't hear me. She wears braces and is too thin and wears too much makeup to cover the acne on her forehead. She is seventeen years old and probably a virgin. She walks into the house and the door closes behind her just as another car pulls into the top of the road. The car is red and driving very fast, too fast for this residential area. It usually takes ninety minutes to drive from Izzie's parents' house to yours, but this is an emergency. At seven I sent Izzie a text from you and then I switch off your phone. To be honest I'm a little surprised Izzie is so eager to come and stop you. I may have underestimated how much of a trainwreck your marriage is but either way she's here, so it's a good job Hannah has nothing better to do with her evening after all.

Your trousers are just about on by the time Hannah runs out of the house and right into Izzie's arms. You manage to turn off the TV but you forget that the computer is on in the other room. You also forget where your greasy pizza fingers have just been foraging and you instinctively put them into your mouth to clean what you think is pizza grease off them and you're yelling at Izzie trying to explain but then your taste buds catch up with you and you vomit all over the laminate floor of the hall and Izzie just slams the door in your face and takes Hannah home.

It takes her thirty minutes even though Hannah lives a few minutes away. When she arrives back at the house she finds the computer still on. The torrented movie is still playing and Starla now has heavy weights attached to her elongated nipples and the hairy hand is pouring candle wax on to her back and her forehead is sweaty and her hair is stuck to it and she's yelling silent screams and her entire body is covered in oozing welts and another woman in high heels starts pissing all over Starla and Izzie picks up the remains of your £250 wine and throws it at the monitor which fizzles and pops. Starla and her tormentors disappear. Izzie watches you for seven minutes as you lie snoring on the floor with vomit in your hair. Unfortunately you had the volume too loud and Hannah never saw what you were doing or where your greaseshit fingers were hiding but hearing Starla from Broomfield Colorado's anguish was more enough for that skinny spotty virgin and she'll be talking about trigger warnings for the next ten years even though she missed the best bit.

Izzie goes upstairs. She takes out a suitcase and puts it onto the bed and I can't believe people really do that it's like a movie and then she stops and looks out the window for a minute the room is dark so I can't really see her face and then she puts the suitcase back into the cupboard and walks downstairs and sits on the sofa and she's got this look and I want to leave the van and go inside and kiss her so much because she finally understands but I can't. That part comes later. Eventually she goes back out to her car and drives away and leaves the front door open. I can just see the top of your head through the doorway so I wait fifteen minutes and let myself in and make sure you're still breathing because now Izzie understands we can't have you checking out yet. I think about putting the wine bottle up your arse but I decide not to and I eat the last slice of cold pizza and stand over you in the dark for about an hour before I decide to call it a night and go back to bed in Number 63.

Izzie doesn't mention the suicide text and persuades you that you invited Hannah over to joke around with her and having only a vague recollection of the night you find it entirely plausible given the state you found yourself and the house in when you woke up the next morning. Izzie makes you pay Hannah £500 and you hand over the cash without saying a word. Then Izzie asks you for another £500 and your eyebrow lifts and she just looks at you and you give it to her. At number 63 I'm grinning from ear to ear. Over the next two weeks that aborted wank costs you £4500, more than Katee ever did. I wonder if you ever think about that when you lie awake at night before the zolpidem and benzodiazepine knock you out.

You haven't eaten pizza since.

Someone leaks Elite & Discreet's unsecured client database on the web. Their clients are livid, and some, valuing their privacy, homicidal. Their London office is firebombed and the Agency's business development manager is found with two bullets in his head in an alley in Budapest. After that, E&D haemorrhage clients. They pay an internet security firm a considerable chunk to find out who is responsible for the hack and a real security firm even more to protect them from their vengeful clients. After a couple of weeks the Agency is in real trouble. Word has spread, and it finds itself unable to attract new clients or retains its old ones. Its rivals sense blood and offer E&D employees a reduction in management fees and a large signing bonus. Within two days three quarters of E&D's young men and women have stopped answering their phones.

E&D's directors hold a meeting. They decide to throw in the towel. But there are a lot of bills. They know some of their creditors will not accept the legal niceties of declared bankruptcy. With only a trickle of money coming in and with wives and mistresses and mortgages and car repayments and cocaine dealers and security and cleaners and administrators and heavies to pay, they decide a quick spot of blackmail is in order. They open their still unsecured file of low risk clients with unusual or embarrassing proclivities and they send them an E&D termination of contract notice that includes a final settlement invoice of £24,950 payable within one week of receipt.

You receive one of these notices and ignore it. Two days later they send you a USB stick containing your secretly recorded entry interview in which you discuss intimate details about your requirements. You ignore that, too. Three days later they send you a picture. You realise you can't ignore it and you ring your credit card company.

Now as someone who blackmails people for a living I have to say that their strategy was a pretty good one, at least for a bunch of beginners in their position. I really can't see how I'd have done it differently given their time constraints. But I'd probably have asked for less money upfront and certainly not stopped at just the one payment. You've got to ease into the thing, you see, otherwise you risk having the target do something stupid. They've got to be able to rationalise it to themselves, justify the expense, otherwise they top themselves or try to run or blubber to their wives or resign from office. Opportunity cost and all that. But you paid and enough others like you paid and Elite & Discreet's indiscretion worked out for them, which is fine by me because that's exactly what I was hoping for when I leaked the client list in the first place.

You fall for Josie within five minutes of meeting her. It's almost too good to be true, a perfect meet cute as they call it in the movies, almost as if it were set up, almost as if that conversation was staged, almost as if someone changed your booking so you'd miss your flight, almost as if someone had doped your takeaway coffee with GHB, almost as if she was standing there at the taxi rank waiting for you, almost as if she dropped her purse at your feet on purpose, almost as if your unimpeded view down the low-cut blouse she happened to be wearing as she scrambled around to pick up the contents of her bag was intentional, almost as if you were supposed to see her wine brochures on the pavement, almost as if she had dyed her hair the exact shade of brown as Katee's, almost as if her glamorous job as a wine buyer were entirely fake, almost as if her entire life was the product of my imagination designed entirely to lure you cock first into a whirlwind romance with a woman you couldn't possibly have had a chance in hell with unless unless unless.
You're welcome.

I head up to tourist spots on the coast and wait for solitary hikers and push them off cliffs. I spike the drinks of kids on holiday in Greece with amphetamines and mention tombstoning and take out a deck chair and watch them plunge to their deaths on the rocks below. I travel to the Alps and do my best Citizen Kane clapping impression. I encourage women to have abortions on online forums. I book cruises and hang around near the railings and wait until the old dears walk by and give them a shove. My record was five biddies on one cruise, which was really something I can tell you, you could *taste* the panic. I break into Spanish villas and take off the pool covers, unfasten the gate, and throw in a teddy bear. I spill oil on the motorway. I cut brake cables at bike racks. I forget to extinguish my cigarettes on long hikes in the woods. I pour cement into storm drains. I break into nursing homes and swap out the heart medication and cholesterol pills for MDMA and LSD. I hack suicide phone lines and give words of encouragement, with examples from history and pop culture. I sell fireworks to minors. I send paranoid schizophrenics photos of their front doors. I go to supermarkets and inject small amounts of mercury into baby food sachets and stab holes in packs of condoms. I leave boxes of matches in playgrounds. I throw ice water over sleeping homeless people in January. I steal life rings. I tamper with fire extinguishers. I tie fishing line at ankle height across the top of escalators. I help old ladies half way across the road. I locate paroled sex offenders and send them detailed maps of nearby schools and bus routes. I visit farms and leave the slurry pit door open. I smear diluted dog shit on ATM keypads. I leave Amanita virosa amongst the loose mushrooms at the farmer's market. I throw children's clothes stuffed with newspapers into rivers. I smash vodka bottles in busy cycle lanes. I buy shares in industrial chemical companies. I seed the Anarchist Cookbook ebook torrent. I apply liberal amounts of peanut oil to nut-free chocolate bar wrappers. I don't cover my mouth when I cough or sneeze. I hide in people's wardrobes and watch them while they sleep and fuck their wives and steal their children.

It had to happen at some point. With a year of gaslighting you the odds of pulling off every single mindfuck clandestinely are pretty slim. I've come to expect it over the years with the dayjob. There's always some angle you didn't see as you're tightening the noose, some chance for the mark to get a good look at your face or trace your bank account or follow you from a drop. You can make as many contingency plans as you want but the real trick is to hit back before they even get a chance to realise that the tables have turned. It's like my old Dad never used to say: hit them fast, hit them low, and hit them hard.
His name is Mike and he works on the same floor as you, six

doors down from your office. He's a VP of something or other, and you've seen him socially on a number of occasions. He's ten years older than you and he drives a Mercedes S-Class and has a different boyfriend for nearly every night of the week.

Unfortunately for Mike he's forgotten his keycard and someone let him in that morning so he doesn't show up on my list when I arrive a little after 11. Even more unfortunately, he's working late, and his midnight visit to the bathroom brings him right past your office where I have, to my shame, left the door ajar. He pokes his head round to say hello to his dedicated co-worker working late into the night but instead he finds me having fun with something or other on your computer and as much as I'd like to pretend I'm with IT, Just doing some network upgrades, I realise from the expression on his face I've left the window blinds open and he can see exactly what is on your three widescreen monitors in the reflection over my shoulder. Mike is not an unworldly man. He knows the distinctive hues and layout of RedTube when he sees it. He knows what an ass grinding up and down on a cock looks like, reflected or otherwise, and if there was any doubt at all, the tinny screams coming from the headphones are enough, and he sets his face to trouble. I try to make a joke out of it but Mike doesn't see the funny side so everything gets very messy very quickly.

So now instead of sitting wanking in your office (in my defence I was waiting for the keylogger to update so thought I'd do a full hard drive rescan and had fifteen minutes to kill so what) I'm driving Mike back to his apartment and we head upstairs and I notice he's left a trail of blood behind us but the door is already opening and his boyfriend of the night is looking at me with jealous eyes and I stab Mike in the kidney and throw him into the room and the boyfriend is built like a fucking wall and he gets me round the throat and the funny thing is the only thing I'm wondering as he's crushing my larynx is where they keep their nail clippers and Mike is so disorientated he rises to his feet and staggers into the back of his boyfriend's knees just enough for the brick wall boyfriend to let go of me for a second and I thrust the knife into his groin and the knife is suddenly slick with blood and I can't pull it out and you get the picture he bleeds out and I manage to take back the knife and nick Mike's carotid but realise the cut looks a bit too clean and a bit too precise so I rake the blade across his neck a few more times and as I watch as their blood pumps out onto the laminate floor and pools around my feet I realise that there's no chance in hell of me making this look like they did it to themselves so I didn't need to worry about nail clippers or clean cuts after all. It takes me all night to clean up. Even if it's not my finest hour I do a good enough job of telling the story that everyone believes they've eloped to South America instead of rotting at the bottom of the North Sea. Most importantly, you're none the wiser. It's almost as if they never existed at all.

At the end of American Psycho (the movie) there's some ambiguity around whether he really is a serial killer after all. There are hints scattered earlier in the movie that he might not be. Dried blood on bedsheets is black, not red. He chases a screaming hooker through an entire floor of an apartment building wielding a chainsaw completely naked except for his Nike trainers and nobody seems to have noticed. But by then you're so invested in seeing what this guy will do next that you don't really think too hard about it and just laugh along with him. But at the end of the movie we're definitely left thinking that it might have just all been in his mind. The lawyer tells him he had dinner with the dead guy in London after Bateman's supposed to have split his head open with an axe to Huey Lewis, but the whole movie is littered with people misremembering names so the lawyer might just be thinking of any yuppie, not the dead one, who really is dissolving in a bath somewhere. But then the dead guy's apartment that's supposed to be full of decomposing hookers is clean when Bateman goes back, and you're not sure if the estate agent is acting weird because Bateman is sweaty and uninvited and peering into cupboards, or because she knows who he really is, what he's looking for, and she's covered it up because it's valuable real estate and she needs the commission and nobody buys apartments where murders have been committed let alone used as cadaver storage however great a view of the Park it has. Then there's that totally implausible chase and shootout with the cops, complete with exploding police cars and overly accurate helicopter searchlights and frantic confession to the lawyer where Bateman admits to killing twenty or forty people and eating their brains and you're not sure if it's real or not. Then finally his pasty secretary finds his diary full of sketches of dead women, and now we're *really* not sure. Was everything we watched just in his head? Did he just imagine killing all those people, the sketches a product of a deranged mind? Nobody can really get away with killing that many people, right? How can he possibly have got away with it all for so long when he's so careless and impulsive and obviously batshit insane?

I don't think I'm really cut out for this kind of life. I was born in the wrong time, wrong place, wrong generation. I like the bigger picture, you know? I like seeing all the moving parts, not just the ones in front of my face. History makes me so depressed. I feel like I'm missing out on something, like the universe has fucked me over. I'd love knowing that if I sign this order five hundred people go into an oven, if I sign that manifesto five million people wearing glasses get their heads hacked off. Now *that's* what I'm talking about. The best of times. Not this amateur shit. I'm not averse to getting my hands dirty by any means. Please don't misunderstand me. I love some of the up-close-and-personal stuff. Watching the little grimaces of pain on your face and the minutely planned events that unfold in the mini soap opera that your life has become is just about the greatest thing you can possibly imagine. I don't want to downplay the immeasurable joy and satisfaction that brings me. But I just wish I was able to put my talents to use on a grander, historical scale. It's like pulling off the legs of ants with tweezers when you can just pour kerosene into the nest and burn the whole fucking lot. I feel like when I was sitting in front of the jobs advisor he gave me the wrong slip. I got construction worker when I should have got architect, or at least concentration camp commander instead of corpse shoveller. I know, delusions of grandeur. But we're all allowed our ambitions. Your ambition is to get out of this mess with both you and your kids still breathing, and mine is to

orchestrate a genocide.
We both can dream, right?

I am not punishing you. You must get out of that mindset. I have no interest in your redemption, your anger, your soul, your desire for revenge. Nor do I want your praise, your pity, your wonder, or your hatred. I am entirely indifferent to what you may or may not think of me. I am only interested in you like I am in a slug writhing around in the salt I've just poured on its back. I watch you with morbid fascination, like a fighting dog in a cage in some Vietnamese shithole. I am a curious observer. I look closely at your wounds. I wonder what your next move might be. Not because I have money on the outcome, but because I enjoy seeing a fish on a hook, an octopus squirming for safety, a baby antelope backed into a corner by a pride of lions. I enjoy seeing the moment the dog knows its fucked and it carries on fighting anyway, teeth bared and jaws gnashing and wet growls until the last crunch of bone, the last whimpered breath. That's all I'm interested in. What your face looks like at the end.

Your daughter's boyfriend, Tom, is a regular Pornhub visitor. I told Sally J__, the school slut, that I'd send pictures of her and her Geography teacher in compromising positions to her parents and the police unless she slept with Tom at a house party. She obliged, as did Tom who, being fifteen, is vulnerable to the advances of anything and everything with tits. That night, I message your daughter about the tryst. Three of her friends verify the liaison. One provides photographic proof of the aftermath. The sight of her Tom and that whore Sally entangled on a sofa surrounded by empty Red Bull cans seems to have unsettled your daughter. I'd switched out her anti-anxiety medication, so she suffers a pretty bad panic attack. I restocked your bathroom cupboard with large quantities of painkillers, your pantry with four bottles of vodka, and your closet with a number of razor blades. I timed the infidelity well: you are at a seminar in Brussels and Izzie is with Sharon and Moll at a spa for the weekend.
I provide the motive and the means and the opportunity. I send

her encouragement by way of a fake message from Tom taunting her sexual frigidity and comparing her cup size unfavourably to Sally's. I settle down in front of my monitors and open a bottle of beer.
But your daughter is made of strong stuff. She does not follow my breadcrumbs, does not go down the rabbit hole. She simply goes to bed and cries into her pillow until Sunday evening when Izzie gets home.
I recycle my empty beer bottle at Tesco two days later.

You're still reading because you think you'll find some way to get yourself off the hook. Oh yes. I know you, remember. Sure, you want to know if your kids are still alive. You want to see which other horrid things that have happened to you and your family in the past twelve months I'm responsible for. You want to see how much more I know about Izzie. These are certainly motivating factors. But we both know deep down that you're only really thinking about yourself. Because I've come along, and now suddenly you can see light at the end of the tunnel. Since I've explained to you what's really going on, you can see a way out. You still think you're cleverer than me. That you'll be able to prove that I ever existed. You think you can show this to the detectives and you'll be off scot-free, wasn't me guv, was the self-confessed serial killer that done it. If not, well, there were extenuating circumstances. It was an aggravated murder. He made me do it. He tricked me. The Terrible Shrinks.
Wrong.
You killed her.
You. No-one else.
You killed your wife, Izzie.
You bludgeoned her and buried her in the forest in a deep grave.
Whatever else happens, you're the only one to blame for that. The blood is on your hands, and all the perfumes of Arabia et cetera.
You should stop worrying about yourself. There's really no point. Forget your little schemes, forget the police, forget any future you're imagining and plots you're hatching. They will not work. And now, for once in your miserable life, stop being a selfish cunt

and think about how the fuck you're going to stop me cutting up your kids, because that's the *best* way this ends.

I'm sitting across from Izzie's work when I decide it's time to stretch my legs and maybe grab a coffee. I've been at it all morning and my legs are going numb. I head down the fire stairs and out through the emergency exit. The weather is bad; cold, damp, and the alley smells awful. Then, as I'm heading towards the road, a woman suddenly appears at my side. My hand is in my pocket and I'm already pulling the blade out before I get a proper look at her.
She's maybe twenty years old, and she's off her head on heroin. Her hair is greasy and there's something wrong about her mouth, and not just because she's gnashing rotten teeth at me. Her eyes are blinking morse code. I take a couple of steps back. Come here she says, grasping for my hand. I shrug her off, and she reaches for me again. Even beneath the H I can see she's touched, foetal alcohol syndrome maybe, or just inbred. I look up and down the alley and drop the blade back into my pocket. My stomach growls, and I can hear the traffic at the end of the alley. I just want a coffee. I tell her to fuck off and turn to go. But she's persistent. She follows me, grabbing for my arm, jabbering on. Look feel this she says, and something about the way she says it, so naive, so trusting, so fucking stupid, that now she's got my attention. I let her take my arm in her filthy scabby hands, and she pulls it quickly toward her stomach, as if I'm going to change my mind. Feel that? she asks and I just look at her, so she presses my hand harder into her swollen belly and I can taste the stench of her dirty clothes in the back of my throat. Then there's this little lurch underneath her T-shirt and she looks up at me and I know then she's not faking. I look up and down the alley again and I realise I haven't left the emergency exit jammed open and I'll have to go around the front to get back into the building which I don't like to do in the middle of the day because there's too many people around and she's still talking and talking and I give her a Robert De Niro glare but not the one you're thinking, I give her the one in *Jackie Brown* when Fonda is winding the shit out of him Lou-*isssssssss* and he turns around and I say Keep your

mouth shut, I mean it don't say one fucking word OK? but she's not paying attention, she's doesn't get the reference, and I gave her a chance but on she goes about how hungry the baby is so I stab her through the eye and drag her body behind the bins and I have to take off my jacket which has a bit of blood on it so I roll it up and put it over her face and then head around to the front of the office block and once inside go straight to the stairs and down to the emergency exit which I remember to prop open this time and drag the body in and wait until it gets dark before I come out again like some nocturnal predator, a leopard maybe, dragging the kill off into the night in my jaws, except I just head to the car with her over my shoulder and drive out to the woods and obviously I don't eat her but I do wonder how long a baby can live inside a corpse and I think of *Alien* and have a bit of a chuckle to myself. The smell of pine trees reminds me of dead bodies now, if you can believe it, I go out there so much, like some fucked up lumberjack Proust pronounced Proost. I buy pine-scented air freshener whenever I'm feeling a bit low. Amazing how strange the brain is isn't it.

I intercepted the photos of your son's birthday, your holiday, and various other snaps taken throughout the summer as Izzie tried to upload them to an online printing company. My regular tech doctors all the photos to make you look fatter than you really are. Izzie doesn't seem to notice, and has three of them framed and put on the mantelpiece. You are enraged but can't say anything without sounding like a vain prick, which you are, so you do.
After the fight you and Izzie don't speak for seventy nine hours and fifteen minutes. The photographs are still on your mantelpiece. I also had the tech narrow your eyes a fraction and make them ever so slightly cross-eyed, just like that dead girl in the alley. If you look really closely, which you do, you look a little bit retarded, which you are.

I killed Hae Min Lee. I was gaslighting Elisa Lam for six months before she took a swim in the water butt. Oh boy was she a crazy kook by the time I was done with her. I forced Gareth Williams to get in that sports bag with the dildo rammed up his ass. I'd go on but you wouldn't believe me. I guess that's up to you.

Your daughter has started to behave so yesterday I move her from the cellar to the room next to mine. Your son carries on playing PlayStation as we walk from the garage up the stairs. She starts to cry a bit when she sees him, maybe because I forgot to tell her he was staying with us or maybe because she's known he's been up here the whole time or maybe because she just misses her brother. Your son doesn't stop playing his game.
Your daughter agrees that she's much more comfortable upstairs. I talk to her for two hours ten minutes about this and that. We talk about you for a while, but mainly we talk about Izzie.

I know what you're dying to ask. Have I told them about Izzie? Have I told them what you did to her? Well I can tell you. No, not yet. But I might. I haven't decided yet. I'm keeping that one in the back pocket for now. We'll just have to see how things work out.

The private detective Elite & Discreet paid to look into Katee's disappearance suddenly starts following you again.
I first notice him while I'm waiting for you to finish up at the gym. He's no Marlowe: he looks like an accountant. He's sitting in a Volvo estate with the driver window cracked. He's smoking. He's parked next to the entrance so he has a good view of people coming and going but he's in enough shadow not to be seen unless you're really looking and even then you'd only maybe get a glimpse of him unless you happened to walk right up to his car and have a long look at him like I did.
I'm curious. E&D has been defunct for over six months, and I'd almost forgotten the business with Katee. I wonder if someone is about to blackmail you again. For once I'm not happy about your impending misery because right at this minute I'm waiting for a few things to come together and this might screw things up. This might make you do something I haven't planned for, and I don't like when that happens.
I know your schedule like the back of my hand and I'm really

only there because it's a nice day and I fancied a break from my Stasi desk. So I ignore you when you come out of the gym with that self-satisfied post-workout shit-eating-grin you always wear and I decide to follow the guy following you. Again, he's no Marlowe: he sits on your tail the whole way between the gym and the bar where you go afterwards to talk about your great workout and drink more calories than you've just burned. He parks three cars down from you and gets out before you've even locked your car. He follows you to the front door of the bar, stops for one minute thirteen seconds while he pretends to talk to someone on his phone, and then goes inside after you.
I open up my tablet and do a bit of digging.
By the time you both emerge two hours seven minutes later I have a bit of a better idea what he's up to. Not-Marlowe's real name is Frank R_. He is fifty-eight years old, twice divorced, and a resident of Nottingham. A former director of Elite & Discreet has got into a spot of trouble (the email didn't elaborate) and has asked not-Marlowe to see if he can scare up some more money from the old list of clients who paid back when E&D folded.
Not-Marlowe is methodical. You are the tenth client he's looking into. According to his notes he'll only pick two or three of the easiest ones to squeeze.
I'm worried because even not-Marlowe will be able to tell you're an easy one.

There's a ridiculous bit in Fight Club in which a young store assistant named Raymond is pulled from behind his counter, taken into an alley, forced onto his knees and told he's about to be shot through the face. This is all supposed to be great fun. Then, just as the turd hits Raymond's pants and he's wondering who will come to his funeral, he gets a reprieve. The gun is removed and he's told he can go, with a warning that if he doesn't turn his life around he'll be hunted down and killed. After Raymond has fled into the night Brad Pitt says that the clerk's breakfast the next morning will be the best he's ever tasted. That when Raymond wakes up tomorrow he'll appreciate his life more than ever before. Armed with this epiphany, this enlightenment, this nobody Raymond will start his life afresh.

The taste of the gun barrel will motivate him more than anything ever has before in his poverty-ridden life to improve his lot, to live the American Dream. Raymond is one lucky guy.

Of course, the idea that the clerk is better off for this encounter is pure nonsense. Utter idiocy. The breakfast might taste fantastic, sure, but poor old Raymond probably suffers from PTSD for the next year and a half and will remember the stink and the shame in his pants for the rest of his miserable, frightened, pathetic life, knowing forever that he's in someone else's debt, that he has to be *grateful* to some psychopathic maniac who could return and strike at any time. Even if Raymond does manage to emerge from the horror of that night and make good on his promise, he'll always know that his ascent up the slippery pole out of his minimum wage existence and into mundane middle class suburbia wasn't because he wanted it. He's *terrified*. He is not any better off. He is not a better person. He has no agency of his own. He can take no personal responsibility for his actions. He's just obeying the reptile instinct to prolong his life as long as possible. And if that means quitting his job and going to night school then so be it.

But there *is* a moment before the nightmares and the therapists and the alprazolam and the outbursts of domestic violence and the panic attacks where it *is* true. Raymond the clerk does wake up and he *does* feel grateful to be alive. Raymond only understood what he had just when he thought he was about to lose it. And for that split second as he hears the gun cock, the psychopath is right. The poor sap does finally appreciate what he has in this world, and he'll do anything, anything, *anything* to keep a hold on it, even if that means throwing away every last shred of autonomy to do it.

Remember that Roald Dahl book? Well there was another part to that story. I kind of stopped part-way through. So here's the next part. So, if you remember, Mr Twit has convinced Mrs Twit that she's got the Terrible Shrinks. But there's a cure, he says. And she says What really? and he says Yes you've got to unshrink yourself and she says But how and he says BALLOONS.

No, there's no balloons. I've thought of something much better for you.

You fly out from Heathrow. By the time you arrive in Barcelona you already look like you want to be back home. I watch your taxi pull up at the hotel. Your son's face is pressed against the window. He's looking for the Nou Camp. He's been talking about it for weeks. He won't get to see it. It won't be the only disappointment of the holiday, nor the worst.
Izzie ushers the children up the steps of the hotel and you follow behind, keeping a suspicious eye on the porter who takes the ramp up from the street level. The two receptionists are talking about you in Spanish as you walk up to the desk, and I think you know it. I stand up from my table and head to the bar where I'll have a better view of you and overhear your room number. Izzie is talking to your daughter, who is saying No I won't do it Mum I won't sleep with him it's weird and he's weird. Izzie is sympathetic. She looks over at you still talking to the receptionist and says to your daughter I'll speak to him and I know she's going to persuade you to share a room with your son, which you'll hate, but this is after the babysitter incident so, just like booking this holiday, you've got no choice in the matter.
You'll never forget that holiday because it was categorically the worst of your life. I can say that quite confidently because you stated it almost every fucking night, as if acknowledging what an awful time you were having might somehow make it less awful (it does not). And the funny thing? I did nothing at all. Not one trick, not one sliver of wood, not one prank or interference or con or hack or text or cancelled taxi or double booking or thieving maid or hired pickpocket or oversalted paella or spiked drink or oversexed neighbour or lost luggage or declined credit card. Sometimes I like to just sit back and watch everything unfold in front of me. I've put all the pieces together, wound up the toy mouse, and it's just ready to all go. All I have to do is let go and watch.
No, that holiday was awful without me lifting a finger. I had nothing to do with your daughter refusing to speak to you, nor the shamefaced expression on your son's face every morning as you made him scrub the urine stains from the sheets. I was

blameless for Izzie's erratic and emotional outbursts, her overindulgence with wine. Even the weather was shite, *in Spain*, as if the universe was determined to make your life a misery for those two interminable weeks.
If your marriage was on the ropes before you left, by the time it was done it was all but dead.
I enjoyed every minute of that trip. It's almost as if your misery is inversely proportional to my pleasure. It made a nice change of pace for me after months of working on you. Even though I couldn't quite stop myself thinking up tricks to pull on you I manage to restrain myself, and it was surprisingly relaxing to let you ruin your own life for a few days. It gave me comfort that if work ever called me away again I could be sure you'd continue down the path I'd set you on, and perhaps even come up with even more ingenious ways to make yourself miserable. That, plus a couple of weeks of restaurant food and hotel amenities really perked me up.
When we land back in the UK I can't wait to get started again. I call up Chloe Josie and tell her to stay clear of you for two weeks, an unexpected expedition to a Chilean vineyard as her excuse, and I don't feel one shred of sympathy for you as you writhe around in bed next to Izzie on those long, interminable, blueballed nights, every morning frantically masturbating in the shower even as Izzie is making you breakfast downstairs, the filthy ungrateful cunt that you are.

It's time for us to move from Number 63.
The kids have been with me a week (how time flies), and I've stayed here longer than I'd planned. I got caught up reading back through my notes and writing all this. I looked up this morning and realised I was slipping behind schedule. I wake your son and unlock your daughter's door and tell them to Get ready, we're going on a trip. Your daughter asks if Izzie will be there (not you I hope you notice) and I say Sort of and she gets that scared look like when she saw Harriet strung up with her neck cut.
We have Cheerios and orange juice for breakfast. I put Taylor Swift on to calm your daughter down but that doesn't seem to work so I switch it off. Your son asks if we can listen to some of

his music and I have to say No, your sister isn't feeling very well, but we'll listen to it in the van and he flashes me this insolent look but I don't say a word, I just let it go.

I cleaned the house last night and packed the bags we needed before I woke them up, so there isn't much left to wipe down. They wait for me next to the garage door. I think I hear green eyes whispering but I pretend to not hear it and finish up.

Your daughter's only fourteen, so I know exactly what she's thinking. I can see the tension in her shoulders. She waits until I unlock the door before she starts to scream. Well, I gave her a chance. Fair's fair. The drugged juice helps. She's already sluggish. I cuff the back of her head with an open palm and she goes down onto the garage floor hard. There's a little bit of blood, nothing serious, just enough to keep her mouth shut until we're clear of the neighbourhood.

Your son makes little sobbing noises as I put her into the back of the van. I have to hold his hand before he'll climb up into the passenger seat. Once we're all strapped in I can smell that he's wet himself, but I don't say anything because I just want to be out the house before sunlight and perhaps he'll learn a valuable lesson sitting in his piss-wet underpants for a couple of hours. Perhaps not. I start the engine and I hear your daughter making whimpering noises through the grate but the engine revs and the garage door opening soon drown that out.

You know that feeling when you've just been hit really, really hard in the balls but the pain hasn't quite started yet? There's pain, yes, but not THE pain, not the pain that gets you all the way up inside and makes you want to puke out your guts. No, that pain always takes a few moments to come, a few seconds of clarity when you know it's about to start and there's nothing you can do but wait for it, knowing that you'll be rolling on the floor tears and snot pouring out your face, clutching your groin like a man possessed imminently, whatever you do. That's the worst part of it, don't you think? That powerlessness. That lucid foretaste of pain, the knowledge that it's about to get a whole lot worse. There's nothing quite like it.

4.

You think snatching your daughter must have been tricky but to be honest it was a cakewalk compared to your son. Abduction is easy, especially when, like Amelie, you have a key. One minute in, a brief scuffle, one minute out, a quick stop at the van and away you go. Piece of piss. Your stupid sister-in-law doesn't hear a thing.
Your son, well, that took a bit more work. There were an awful lot of moving parts. Wheels within wheels like you wouldn't believe. I won't bore you with the details.
Actually, yes I will.
We're talking months of work preparing the ground, sowing the seeds. To turn a normal, healthy twelve year old boy into a kid with extreme suicidal ideation is difficult. I mean, really fucking *hard*. You're easy compared to that. I just need to send you an email or prank call you or fuck your wife and I can see the smoke coming out of your ears. This was completely different. Grooming on a massive scale. Those paedophiles trawling social network sites and creating fake profiles and listening to One Direction have nothing on me. I had to arrange every single thing your son saw. I prompted and nudged and coaxed and bullied and manipulated for hours and hours and hours every day. I had to get his best friend excluded from school. I had to make him hate you (easy) and Izzie (fucking hard, especially with that Oedipal thing he had going on). I wrote thousands and thousands and thousands of words extolling the virtues of death, evoking ennui and eliciting existential crises in a *twelve year old*. I didn't even have the hormones of full blown puberty to help me. Except for some mild narcotics I managed to lace his cereal with, that was all *me*. I sent him countless messages, recommended scores of films and games and bands, created a whole network of self-reinforcing teens he could talk to. I hacked his browser so that whenever he typed suicide into Google none of those hotlines

turned up. I had to prevent him going on those chat rooms where they talk you down and post inspirational bullshit, keep him away from those Golden Gate Bridge regret stories. We're talking some serious puppet master type shit. I once had a five hour conversation about painless methods in a private suicide chat room where I was playing four different kids. My hands ached for two days afterwards.

I even created his very own suicide buddy, Carly, a fifteen-year old mix of temptress and angsty self-loathing dropout who I used to buck your son up, turn him on, or make him feel utterly worthless as and when.

Then, just when Carly is going to suggest a trip to the woods to leave all his problems behind, you go and lose your temper and instead of a dead son you've got a dead wife.

I can't emphasise enough how much you messed up my plans. This is just a small example; we're talking about a whole campaign that you screwed up. Idiot.

In the end I had to call Chloe. She doesn't exactly sound what I imagined Carly to sound like but she's the best I could come up with at such short notice. Your son is so excited about finally talking to Carly on the phone that he doesn't even notice. He agrees within two minutes. I'm not sure whether he was completely ready, whether he really would have gone through with it or not. I guess it doesn't really matter. Knowing that your twelve year old son skipped school to fondle a girl he thinks is fifteen but is actually your stalker is nowhere near as good as him heading out into the woods and hanging himself from a tree with a plastic bag full of helium tied around his head, but it's the best I can do at the last minute.

He gets off the school bus two stops early and I can see him looking around for the white van. Your son is horny, so he hasn't figured out that fifteen year old girls rarely drive any kind of vehicle, and especially not white vans. I watch the bus head off and a few kids' heads turn to look. When the road is quiet again I start the engine and slowly roll up alongside him. He tries to peer through the windows but they're blacked out. But he still opens the back door and gets in, just like Carly told him to. I get a thrill out of that. Even if I couldn't get him to end it all in the woods I can still make him get into the back of a strange van with almost no effort at all. Just one phone call. And like that, poof. He's gone. I hear him pull the door closed behind him and I hit the lock button on the dash. I drive him back to Number 63 and he barely makes a noise when I open the van door. Maybe he always knew it was too good to be true. I smile at him and we have a long talk and he catches on pretty quick. Funny that. He must have got that from Izzie.

Talking of Izzie.
You must be wondering by now how someone like me could have possibly managed to joke around with her three times. You think it's a lie (it isn't). She can't exactly protest her innocence, can she? You think I'm manipulating you. You think I'm talking about joking around with her to fuck with you. To enrage you. The Terrible Shrinks. The Perceived Hollow. You think it's another one of my tricks, another sliver of wood on the walking stick. That, or I must have made her do it. Forced myself on her, threatened her, gave her no choice but to sleep with me.
Well, you're right. She didn't have a choice.
And now you're maybe feeling a bit relieved. You're thinking Oh thank god, she was just drugged and raped and sodomised. She never had a choice. And that makes you feel better about yourself, even though you bludgeoned her and left her to rot and it shouldn't matter either way. But of course it does. Fucking someone is one thing, but being raped? Well, that could happen to anyone. She didn't have a choice, did she? She was forced against her will. She might have been a lot of things but At least she never chose to sleep with this monster who has ruined all of our lives. She's not to blame. She's a *victim*, just like you. Poor Izzie.
You make me sick.
She didn't have a choice because, like your son, she was so horny she could hardly think straight. There was no rational choosing between yes and no. She wanted it so badly, she was so wet, that she let me fuck her three times (once in her ass, no times with a condom).
And now you're mad again. You don't believe me. We're right

back at the beginning. So here you go, here's the story that you will believe.

His name isn't Magnus but we'll call him that. Magnus is 192cm tall and if I tell you to picture a Norse demigod you'd still be missing the mark. This man is unbelievable. I found him in a casino in Monaco, surrounded by men and women who all had that look in their eye. He's got wavy blond hair, bright blue eyes, dimples; the works. I could go on but you get the picture. Magnus is the kind of guy who can make other men throw tens of thousands of dollars away at the tables to impress him as they try to conceal their confusing erections behind their whisky sodas. As for the women, well, you can almost hear their cunts churning and their thighs squelching as they encircle him. An aura of moisture and envy and lust and tuna seems to follow him around wherever he goes.

Like I said, he is perfect.

Magnus isn't the only honeytrap we employ but he is without a doubt the best. We keep him on retainer for the most exclusive and difficult jobs, and he's our most expensive contractor by a huge margin. You see where I'm going here. I could tell you a hundred stories about his exploits but I guess you're impatient for the climax, right?

Izzie is careful, unlike you. No Travelodges and escort agencies or golf bags for her. She's a model of discretion. She waits until the weekend, preferably one where you are on a trip. She selects one of her evening dresses, usually a little black number, unlocks the safe, 5665, puts on her expensive jewellery, drives to an ATM, takes out £500, then heads to either the B__ Hotel or I__ bar. She orders a glass of white wine or a cocktail, oftentimes a Mojito. She drinks three glasses before she looks around at the other patrons, and she rubs the backs of her fingers against her flushed cheek and makes eyes at the best looking one. She prefers chestnut brown hair, simple but expensive-looking shirts, tight trousers, and long eyelashes. Izzie enjoys one of these nights perhaps once every couple of months, although I notice they increase in frequency in the last six months of my campaign to maybe two or three times a month, whether you were out of the country or not.

That night I follow her to I_ bar and I head inside after about fifteen minutes. Magnus is already there, waiting, like a spider. He's been in the country for two weeks ready just for this moment. I won't tell you what that cost me. I walk up to the bar and glance around to see where he is. Izzie is still on her first cocktail and hasn't noticed him yet. He's in the back, surrounded by four women who are looking up at him with wolfish eyes. He sees me and I turn away, take my phone out of my pocket and send him the message. I order a drink, wander to a table at the back, and watch him work his magic.

I've got a really good view of Izzie's face so when he sits down on the stool next to her I can see that little frown of annoyance she gets. The fire hasn't started in her belly yet, and unlike you she needs a bit of liquid courage. I can see her just about to rebuff the premature intruder. Her hand is already in the air, her mouth about to tell him to buzz off, when she looks up from the drink. Magnus knows exactly how to act. I've seen him work plenty of times so I can focus all my attention on Izzie. He always takes care to be looking away when they first get a glimpse of him, preferably in profile. He lets them gape for about three seconds, then he slowly looks back at them. There's a flash of perfect white teeth, his cheeks dimple, and those little perfect creases form around his eyes, and then he looks away to give them time to recover. It sounds corny when I write it down but believe me it never fails. He's demure and charming and smouldering and everything a woman could ever want in a man. Seriously I can't emphasise enough how much better looking he is than you. I wish I have infrared goggles on because the blood must be pouring into Izzie's groin. He introduces himself, buys her a drink, and she can't keep her eyes off him. Like she can't quite believe he's real. I wonder if she's comparing him to you as her eyes eat him up. Probably not. She doesn't look like she'd even remember your name. She downs the cocktail fast.

And then comes part two.

Part two is tricky because she isn't quite drunk enough yet and, well, next to movie-star Magnus, I'm a nobody. Invisible. So when Magnus calls me over after about half an hour and introduces me as his good buddy she hardly takes her eyes off of him to glance at me. Her hand is clammy and I hold on to it for a fraction too long. She looks back at me for a split second. There's no hint of recognition even though I've been following her for months. Then Magnus says something and Izzie is gone again, lost in those blue eyes. We talk for a bit longer, and as Izzie is draining another Mojito I see Magnus nod. It's imperceptible to everyone but me. I know he's right. She's in the bag. The hard part is over. Two more drinks, maximum, and she'll be ready. Magnus practically has to wipe the drool off his shoulder.

When they went into Jeffrey Dahmer's apartment all they found in the fridge was a decapitated head and assorted condiments. That was it. American Psycho does a riff on it. Instead of mustard, Bateman's fridge has posh ice cream next to the severed head. Nice bit of class consciousness that I appreciated. But I think it says something interesting about Dahmer. He's a poor guy. He lives in a shitty neighbourhood, works in a chocolate factory, rides the bus to work, drinks too much. There's a famous home video of him before anyone finds the bodies where his Dad mentions that Dahmer's gran has noticed he's lost a bit of weight, and Dahmer replies saying I've been eating a lot of McDonald's but it's really expensive so I'm having to eat at home more now. Everyone likes that because we know he was eating people, ha ha what a crazy coot. But I like it for a different reason. Because maybe the cannibalism was just him being resourceful, you know? Trying to make sex zombies by drilling holes into their skulls and pouring water and chemicals directly into their brains has a lot of trial and error to it. It leaves you with a lot of bodies, for a start. And like I said Dahmer is poor, he can't afford to eat at McDonald's, he lives in a tiny apartment in a rough neighbourhood surrounded by drug dealers, and by the way he's also an alcoholic. So why not supplement the diet with a bit of human protein? There's plenty of it hanging around the place. Why the hell not? They're going to die anyway: Dahmer needs his sex zombies, after all. It makes no difference to them. And for Dahmer it's added value, a two-for-one deal, a Happy Meal with a cheeseburger and the toy soldier to play with. Besides, a man's gotta eat. So if I have to fuck your wife three times once in the ass no times with a condom as part of my plan to destroy your life then it's pretty much the same thing, right? It's just a perk of the job, like Dahmer's Happy Meal.

I can see Izzie isn't exactly enthralled by the idea at first but whenever she's about to buck Magnus knows what to do and I can literally see her knees wobble whenever he brushes his hand against her neck or whispers into her ear. The trick is the *positioning*. As long as her head's facing Magnus and she can see those eyes and that face and that body of his I can pretty much go nuts with the rest of her. We have a very good night and the funny thing is even though I get to know Izzie really really really well I bet she wouldn't even remember what I looked like. I'm not offended. She made all the right noises and I certainly enjoyed myself.

The problem is, after being with Magnus, you just won't ever cut it again. Now maybe you understand what changed between you, why your long slide into mutual indifference dropped off a fucking cliff into mutual *hatred*. Yup, that was me and my pal Magnus and our very wild night three times one time in the ass no times with a condom, and believe me Magnus had plenty of fun with the top end too. Sorry about that. You never did manage to sleep with her again after that night.

Izzie's parents visited you today and I had to stop everything I was doing to watch. It was truly entertaining stuff. Your father-in-law looks very old all of a sudden, sort of ashen sombre gaunt, and he just stares at you with Auschwitz orphan eyes like he's not sure of anything anymore. Your mother-in-law rattles on and on about the police and the detectives she calls by their first names and all her friends that have called and written and baked for them and then suddenly she just goes really quiet when she mentions your daughter's name and there's this really long, awkward pause and I can see you grimacing and I think you're trying to work out how to act and I really really really want you to ask them if they've started work on their kitchen yet but I was wrong and I guess maybe you're actually pretty shook up yourself about the kids and you cry for the first time since I took them and I can tell it's not a cynical thing because there's snot pouring from your nose and you're making these hysterical little gurgling noises and I'm crying along with you because Izzie's parents aren't quite sure whether you're about to confess or not and they won't touch you they just sit on the sofa watching you and then they excuse themselves and you kind of slump forward with your head in your hands and stay like that for nearly an hour. All this time I thought you were going to take the easy way out of this. But now I'm wondering whether actually despite the mess with Izzie and the fact that you've hardly ever shown any inkling that you even like your kids let alone love them that maybe there is something there. Maybe you are actually really torn up about it and I shout aloud I'm so happy, so happy that all that fucking work isn't going down the drain tantus labor non sit cassus.[2]

Chloe Josie has you over her knee. You're too easy. She's managed to reduce the number of times you see her to once a fortnight, if that, and you're so excited when she does finally grant you an audience in one of her apartments around Europe you're over and done with in less than ten minutes. It might just be the easiest £50k a month of Chloe's life, especially when you consider that I'm the one you are messaging every night. But I don't mind her drawing such a big salary, even if all she has to do is fuck you and wash up the wine glasses afterwards.
You only tried to pull out your golf bag once, and she shot you down so fast you couldn't get it up again all night. No funny business with Chloe. She's no tramp, no Katee. You think you're in love, but I don't think Chloe even knows your surname, and she had no idea about your plans for elopement. That was all me, honey bun.

Everyone seems convinced that somehow, some way, they'll be the ones to survive. Whatever it is, they'll pull through. War, pandemic, nuclear apocalypse, zombies. They're never going to

---

[2] EN: "May such great work not be in vain." Mozart, *Requiem Mass* in D minor (1791), "Dies Irae" Movement.

be the ones to bite the dust. Not *me*, they say. Sure, it'll be difficult, and Maybe I'll have to do some tough things to survive, Some things I might have nightmares about, But I'm going to survive. It's like they can't quite picture themselves dead. They'll find the fallout shelter, they'll be immune, they've got the summer house in the hills by the stream, they've got a cupboard full of baked beans, they have waterproof matches, they don't even live anywhere near an army base, they can run four kilometres without stopping once. Death is completely out of the realm of their understanding. Just try it. Go on. Imagine yourself dead. And I don't mean theoretically. No bright white lights or dark nothingness to escape into. I mean actually picture your dead body lying sprawled awkwardly on the floor, your eyes glassy, your lungs still, your teeth clenched, your flesh cold as a slab of meat in the fridge. Try to picture the exact moment when the sound of you beating heart will no longer be going on inside your head. Tough, right? You try to picture someone else, certainly not your face and your body and your clothes.

Well I need you to really have a good long think about it. I need you to really understand it, and when I say understand it, I mean *accept* it.

Got it? Okay. Good.

Now we're getting somewhere.

Not-Marlowe is sniffing around far too much for my liking. He's clocked you for what you are, and his focus for the past couple of weeks is almost exclusively on you. I don't like that. You're *mine*. I spend a lot of time watching him watching you. I know I have to be careful. Private detectives keep lots of notes, have lots of backups. I can't just bump him off. Somehow I have to make him forget all about you, make him move along to someone else.

I can't have that kind of uncontrolled risk buzzing about after so much work. There's too much exposure and I have to implement some risk mitigation strategies, if you like.

It's funny what can make a person snap, to go postal, to run amok, to strap on the C4 and whip out the AR-15 and mount the pavement. That's actually a medical term, you know. To Run

Amok. It's a real thing, not just an expression. A psychological condition. Anyway, with you the infidelity was a factor, but if you think like that then so were Mr Taylor's roosters or your son screeching Slender Slender Slender at you. They got you close, yeah, but none of things actually pushed you over.
No, that was the diary.
I almost didn't write the thing. It seemed like a waste of time. I guess I didn't know you as well as I thought I did.

I followed you to the hotel. The whole time I never really thought you'd go through with it. I reckoned you'd sit brooding outside for a bit, hoping to catch sight of her at the window. Maybe you'd storm in and make a scene. You were so poorly prepared, I honestly didn't think you'd do it. How can I have known? I didn't think you could be *dumb* enough. I know. Joke's on me, right? I've watched you for twelve months and you *still* have the ability to shock me with your pig-headed stupidity. If I'd known what you were actually going to do, well, I might have run you off the road. Planning: zilch, zip, zero. No body bag, no alibi, no cutting tools, no change of clothes, not even a plastic sheet for the car. It is all so impulsive. So ridiculous. So *mundane*. You even stop at a service station, buy a BLT sandwich, a bag of prawn cocktail crisps and a Pepsi, and eat in your car next to the parked lorries. How was I supposed to know you could be that cold-hearted? That you were the kind of person to that could eat a soggy sandwich, throw a half-drunk Pepsi out your window, then drive for another forty minutes to the hotel your wife was staying at, sneak inside and bludgeon her to death without so much as an exit strategy?
And don't try to tell me it was an accident, a moment of madness, a jealous rage. Things got out of hand. Bullshit. I saw the hammer. You got out of the car with it. It was only then that I realised what you had in mind, only then did I understand. Maybe I could have done something then, but maybe not. Maybe I was already thinking of the next way to hurt you. A new way to end my campaign. Strange how easily I slotted Izzie's death into my plans, isn't it? After that night with Magnus I had a bit of a thing for her. Maybe you've realised that by now. What can I say.

I'm a pragmatist. You've got to roll with the hammer blows, right?

Izzie's smoking on the balcony of her room and I see you behind her. The room is lit up like a fucking casino and I don't even need my binoculars. It's a good job no-one else is in the car park or you'd be done for. You hit her twice on the head. She goes down without making a sound. I wince at the blood spatter. That's going to take at least an hour to clean up. You spend a bit of time with her body (we've all been there), and I think you're going to be sick but you man up and just throw her over the railing into the bushes below. It's a good job its one of those expensive country hotels, surrounded by trees and shrubbery, and the lighting is less utilitarian and more decorative. She lands squarely in a big bush with very little noise, and in the dim light you can barely see her and only then if you're really looking. Can you imagine throwing a body out of a Travelodge window? But anyway you take fifteen minutes before you come out the fire exit and I'm getting antsy. Almost like I'm rooting for you, you know? You've come this far, it'd be such a shame if someone happened to be looking outside and saw Izzie sprawled out in the rhododendron with her skull caved in. You're struggling with her bag and you look over at my car but you don't stop, you're walk-running to your car and throw the suitcase into the boot and then you drive up as close to the bush as you can and you half-roll and half-drag her into the back seat. More evidence. You close the door quietly, NOW YOU'RE CAREFUL, and you don't stop, you're in the front seat and then gravel flies everywhere. I sigh because I have a lot of cleaning up to do and because you're an idiot. I watch your lights as they wind down the track until they disappear into the darkness. Then I put my gloves on and get out my bag and I get to work. Let's get down to brass tacks gentlemen I almost say under my breath.

You laugh at TV adverts. *Out loud.* And definitely not ironically. Not just a snort, either. Not even a chuckle. A proper *laugh.* Moron.

You've done a piss poor job of cleaning up after yourself so I'm only about halfway done when you remember her Audi. I'm on the balcony cleaning up Izzie's hair and blood where you left it splattered everywhere and I see your car drive up. I'd recognise those blue-white LEDs anywhere. I duck back into the shadows and wonder what the fuck you're up to.

You've only been gone about twenty minutes, and unless you're really really stupid that's not long enough to hide a body by any stretch of the imagination. I realise you've just driven back to the crime scene and *Izzie is still in the back of your car.* Genius.

You prowl around a bit in the car attracting attention with that stupidly overpowered engine and then you get out and walk over to Izzie's Audi around the side of the hotel where I can't see you. Then you drive back around front in it, too fast. It's like that story with the fox and the rabbit and the beans except it's an Audi a body and an idiot. I open up my tablet and follow the GPS signal from her car and you only go a couple of miles up the road and I see you stop at what looks like a small farm and then about thirty minutes later you come jogging up the track again. Somehow, somehow, somehow nobody has noticed you. I think about what I should do to you if you come up to her room and I'm ready to really hurt you and I'm looking around for something to gag you with but instead you just poke around in the bushes underneath the balcony where you dumped her body and then you're gone again, this time for good, off to bury your wife.

There's another Roald Dahl story I like. This old bachelor finds out about this portrait painter who convinces all these rich society women to pose naked for him so he can better capture their figures. Pretty crafty, right? They go right along with it. They sit for him over three sessions. At the first session he paints them in the nude. At the second session they pose for him in their underwear (corsets and girdles et cetera), and he paints these on top of the nude figure. Then finally comes the fully clothed session, and he adds the evening gowns and jewellery on top in a final layer of paint.

Our old bachelor has a good chuckle at this. He admires the gumption of this painter who manages to get all these women to strip down for him in the name of art, amazed at how easily these gullible women swallow the bullshit story about the three layers of paint.

Anyway, a bit later in the story our bachelor finds out that the woman he's been sleeping with has been talking shit about him all over town. Now this guy is a worldly man. He's been around. He's in his sixties, and he must have slept with hundreds of women in his time. But when he hears this woman has been talking about him behind his back, saying things like He's so boring and He's so predictable, things like that, it makes him mad. Really, really mad. He's fuming. This perfectly normal man is absolutely enraged by these fairly trivial comments, which he's heard from a fairly dubious source, to the point where he considers killing her. Can you imagine that? To be so livid about what someone might have said about you that you could actually want to *murder* them?

In the end the bachelor doesn't kill her. He's not a cretin. Instead, he has this brilliant idea. You might have guessed it. He keeps quiet, and then he commissions the crafty painter, him with the three sessions, one in dishabille, one in drawers, one in dress, to paint his lover, who is none the wiser. When our bachelor gets his hands on the finished portrait of his lady friend he carefully removes the top two layers of paint to reveal his lover in a rather unflattering light, warts and girdles and saggy tits and all. An old-worldy version of revenge porn, if you like. He invites his lover and all their society friends around for a dinner party, and at this big gathering of the great and the good he reveals this modified portrait of her. He gets his revenge. She's mortified. He stays for just long enough to see the look on her face (a man after my own heart. I told you Dahl was a writer for people like me).

Now, if only *you* could have been smart enough to think of something like that. But no. You read the diary, swallowed it hook line and sinker, went to the shed, got a hammer and drove to the hotel she was staying at and hit her with it like the fucking caveman that you are. Poor Izzie. She didn't even keep a diary. How could you not know something like that? How can you have been fooled so easily by such an obvious fake? I barely even disguised my writing.

It's okay though, because the woman in Dahl's story gets her revenge. She writes the crusty old bachelor this long sweet note forgiving him, which makes the old man realise what an utter cad he's been. She's even good enough to send him his favourite treat, caviar, to show there are no hard feelings. The man, consumed by guilt, wolfs it down, never suspecting how utterly implausible it would be for her to ever forgive him for publicly humiliating her like that. It turns out the caviar is a bit rich for our old bachelor. He's only had a few mouthfuls and he's suddenly feeling very unwell, actually really very poorly, and he's got nobody to blame but himself.

I like it because you've been in a quandary ever since I took your kids. When I saw your face going into the police station I thought you'd ruin it all, just start spouting, but the police were good enough to make the conclusion for you. When they laid it out you just go with it. Yes Izzie is missing, Yes she probably did take the kids now that you mention it Yes we were having some troubles at home Yes I think she did have some affairs Yes Officer your story is the only one that makes any sense and now it's too late to change your story even if you could come up with a better one.
A few things are helping us. The fact that your sister-in-law definitely saw your daughter that morning and his schoolmates distinctly recall seeing your son getting on and then off the bus alone helps because you have a solid alibi for that morning. I made sure of it. You were on a video conference call the whole time and it was recorded and fifteen colleagues across Europe can verify you were there picking your nose and looking bored the entire time. Besides, your car never left the car park, your secretary confirms you were in the office with the door locked on the fifteenth floor and Poirot Marple Columbo Jessica Fletcher combined couldn't pry that one apart in a month of Sundays.
So there's five ways the police think it could have gone down:
The Sleeping With The Enemy theory: Izzie, fleeing an unhappy and/or abusive marriage, perhaps with a lover, took the kids.
The They Knew Too Much theory: The kids run away after you killed Izzie, perhaps having seen you do her in.

The Dial M For Murder theory: You arranged for someone else to kill/abduct your wife and kids, whilst organising a perfect alibi for yourself.

The One-Armed Man theory: A stranger took Izzie and the kids from three separate locations with no witnesses and no sign of a struggle.

The Shannon Matthews theory: You and Izzie have colluded to fake her disappearance and your children's kidnapping in an elaborate attempt to make her parents or your insurance company pay out against a large ransom demand.

I've listed those in the order the police think the most likely, according to your case file, though their theory names aren't as good as mine and I've summarised a bit. They do a lot of digging and it's a good job I hid those extortion withdrawals for you because the police could jump to all sorts of conclusions and you'd be in a whole lot of pain right now, you should be grateful, by the way you are now the proud owner of a very nice yacht named *The Katee II* you're welcome.

The police are fairly certain it's the Jilted Husband AKA Sleeping With The Enemy theory. The police like to look at *evidence*, and I've left so fucking much of it they're tripping over themselves to come to a conclusion that doesn't involve a triple murder investigation. Izzie is missing, there's history of marital discord and infidelity, the kids seemed to have gone willingly, Izzie has an exit plan that involves flight from the country, there's withdrawals and charges on her accounts and someone is driving her car around and she's sent emails to close relatives and divorce lawyers hours and days after she and the kids went missing. It all stacks up, even if it scares the shit out of you.

The second theory, They Knew Too Much, is a possibility but I've made it really complicated for them to find a crime scene and even though you're acting really strangely they seem to put it down to worry over your missing kids and you have fooled them about Izzie, at least for now. Don't get me wrong, there's a couple of detectives that are dying to pin it on you, but like I said, *evidence*. The narrative of it makes no sense, there's too many moving parts, too many weird little coincidences and dead ends and confusing contradictory evidence.

So the absolutely worst thing for you to do is mention that a stranger took your kids. Because it makes you look guilty, makes you look insane, makes you look like a liar, especially because so much of your story relies on Izzie being alive and breathing to take them. The kids deflect all the attention from what you did or didn't do to her that night. If Izzie didn't take the kids then where the hell is she buster?
You have no choice but to keep your mouth shut. But I guess if you've read this far you already know that.

I'm not really a fan of burial as a method of disposing a body. It's hard work. Much harder than you realise when you pick up the shovel from B&Q and head out into the forest thinking Oh, sure, this can't be too difficult, just a small trench, like digging a flowerbed over, and then you realise how fucking big and deep you've got to make it and even if you fold or cut up the body we're still talking a good few hours of work if you don't want animals digging her up and bear in mind you're doing this in the middle of fucking nowhere it's dark and you only have a crappy torch and the ground is full of roots and rocks and you've forgotten to bring gloves and you'd be better off with a pickaxe not a garden shovel and by the time you're halfway done your clothes are soaked right through with sweat and you're feeling all shaky especially now the adrenaline is gone but it's not like you can come back and finish it off the next day after a hot meal and nice long bath, can you?
Me? I just hire a digger. One of those mini ones. So much easier. You were in the woods burying Izzie for six hours all told, and I dug her out of there in just under ten minutes. The hardest part wasn't even finding where you'd buried her. The GPS gave me a good idea, and for the record you should never drag a body. Far too conspicuous. No, the hardest part was getting the ten metres off the forest track to the place. I'm smart, though. I have a chainsaw. I only needed to take three trees down to get access. I was in an and out in an hour. Simple, really, when you think about it.

I drive to your garage and make sure I get all the evidence I need.

Izzie's suitcase, the murder weapon, your blood-spattered clothes, the lot. Another bartering chip, in case you don't value your children's lives all that much. I give the plastic wrap around Izzie's body another once over before I take everything out to the cottage and dump it.

This won't stop.

It's been two days since we moved from Number 63. Your daughter seems to have settled down again, and your son has even perked up a bit, especially when I introduce the dog. I think your daughter realises what he's there for but your son is still a bit young to realise that dogs are like people, there are good ones and bad ones, and some really bad ones that just pretend to be good ones until they hear a certain word or someone happens to stray too far from the house and then you'd be surprised at how quickly they lose that friendly look and how expertly they can turn you inside out. The cottage isn't as secure as Number 63 but I can still spend time away from the house with the dog there, which is good because there's still plenty to do.

Maybe you'd be surprised to learn that I'm not a particularly practical person. Sure, I can handle the tools of my trade. Knives, guns, poisons, are all fine. If I have to cut up a body I can do it no problem. I guess what I mean is that I'm not very *handy*. I can pick a lock, but I never could change the oil or put up a bookcase. I never really liked the Saw movies, for example. Not just because they are preachy and they sucked but because there was just too much *engineering*, if you know what I mean. Too much fucking about with screwdrivers and welders and angle grinders coming up with those contraptions. Operating the excavator to dig up Izzie is about the extent of my manual skills, and I could only do that because it's like a computer game, they even have those little joysticks to operate them. I much prefer my engineering *social*, and I'm not too proud to admit it either.

So getting things ready for you was going to take me a while, because I have to watch YouTube videos before and during and sometimes after and I have to go step by step and I get the wrong screws from B&Q three times and it has to be perfect so it takes me over a week doing a job I guess one of my specialists, one of my heavy lifters, could have done in maybe two days if I thought I could trust them to do it for me. Afterwards looking at it I feel kind of proud of myself and the kids haven't been any trouble. You'd hardly know they're here, although I kind of miss watching you a bit even if you're mainly just moping around the house drinking too much.

So here's what's going to happen. I hope you haven't skipped to this part because it's taken me a lot of hours to type all this out. If you have, well, what a surprise. Oh, and fuck you. Always looking for the easy road aren't you? You've spent your whole life like that and look where it's got you. So go back and read every fucking word you stupid cunt, because if you don't you won't realise how fucking serious I am and how fucked you are if you don't do exactly as I tell you.
You have two options:

Actually you know what? I'm going to make you wait a bit longer for it. Work for it. I don't think you're ready yet. I don't think you really understand yet.

So the Chinese water torture is pretty good, but there's plenty of other methods you could use on, say, a child if, say, you wanted to make their parents do something.[3]

You spend nearly six hours at the police station. Your phone battery cuts out after about an hour so I don't get to hear the whole interview, but I've got a pretty good idea of what they're thinking. I realise I still need to take care of a few details, so I leave you to your amateur dramatics and I head out to clear some of them up.
You seemed to think that leaving Izzie's Audi in long-term parking at the airport is a *good* idea. It really isn't. I head over there and pick it up and drive it down to Folkestone, where I've

---

[3] EN: The next three paragraphs have been removed as being too disturbing for publication. See *Editor's Afterword* for further discussion of this excision.

booked three tickets on the ferry to Calais. They'll check the cameras so I drive around for a while making sure the seat is as far back as it'll go. Then I use Izzie's credit card to book a hire car in Calais, and two nights in a guest house in Rouen, and then a bit later three bus tickets to Plymouth and one adult two children train tickets to Glasgow to really fuck with them. That should be enough to throw them off your trail for a while at least, given you're sat in D_ police station while I'm doing all this. You really ought to be grateful.

The rest is pretty easy. A few fake emails to colleagues, her sister, and a divorce lawyer, a rejected cash withdrawal at a garage in Wolverhampton, some changes to mobile phone records (yours and hers), a lot of confusion about which hotel and which room she was staying at the night you murdered her, a phone call the morning after you killed her to a Barcelona hotel, and some other stuff that will keep the police thinking she's still alive and has the kids with her and that she's walked out on you. Nothing complicated, just confusing. No need to call in any of my team. I only need about three weeks, after all. It only has to be convincing enough for them to let you out, otherwise the whole thing has been a complete waste of time.

I guess you probably don't believe me. Maybe you think your kids are already dead. You think I'm just tormenting you. And if they're not dead then I've done something really horrible to them.

Well I haven't. In fact, I can tell you exactly where every scratch, every bruise, every swelling is. And now you're thinking how could I know where every scratch bruise swelling is unless unless unless but don't be stupid I'm not your brother after all I can control myself. I'm not a *monster*. That one time doesn't count. I defy you *not* to lick a pussy hand thrust under your nose in the dark. Can you honestly say you wouldn't? Liar. Lying liar.

Anyway there's been nothing like that here, I can tell you, I've been much too busy like I said making preparations et cetera. So here's the list:

Your son has one small cut under his left eye where he fell over whilst playing with the dog and caught his cheek on the coffee

table. No harm no foul.
He's put on maybe three or four kilos since he's been with me. He really likes his MaccyD's and Meat Feasts.

Your daughter is about six kilos lighter than when I took her, give or take half a kilo.
She has a series of small red marks on her right wrist where she tried unsuccessfully to open up the artery with a butter knife which believe me I quickly put a stop to and you can hardly blame me for.
She has a bruise on her neck where I cuffed her with my palm when she tried to escape that time I told you about already.
She has a slightly bigger bruise and a bit of swelling above her right eye where she hit the garage floor.
She has some other minor bruising on her right forearm, left ankle, cheekbone, both thumbs, collarbone, breastbone, tailbone and right thigh. Like I said, she's a squirmer.
She has a very small dog bite, really very minor, on her groin where she went a bit too far from the house and the dog had to remind her about boundaries.
She has some slight hair loss above her right ear and around her temple where she's been pulling out her hair, mostly at night I think because I've never seen her do it but I find it in in her bed when I tidy and check the rooms in the mornings.

See? They're fine.

Nobody has said anything to your face. Everyone's so fucking *polite*. Your sister-in-law is telling everyone she knows that you've got something to do with it and that Izzie would never run off with someone else and especially not without saying something to her family first but it's all very English and nobody wants to be the first to point the finger.
So I do.
I drive over to your house which is risky as hell but fuck it and I paint those words on your car which you spend hours trying to clean off but give up in the end and call a taxi to Halfords and get your own spray paint to cover it up but not before most of the

neighbours have seen and that's enough for me. I notice that you've changed the locks since I left Number 63 which I must have missed on the cameras. Like I said, I've been very busy. But the changed locks are interesting because it means you've finally realised that, no, the kids didn't run off, someone else was definitely involved, and that means we're one step closer.

So just when I think your daughter understands we go right back to square one. I literally wrote that part listing all the bruises swellings cuts the kids have and I decide to take a quick break for lunch and she makes a liar out of me within an hour. She's been hiding food again, slipping it up her sleeve when I'm not looking. I saw her doing it out the corner of my eye. Your son must have known she was doing because we all sit at the table together to eat. I had to take away his PlayStation privileges for a day and send him to bed without tea or ice cream. You have to be firm but fair. As for your daughter I sat her down and wiped my hands with a dishcloth and I said IS IT SAFE and she remembered but instead of showing her *Marathon Man* I turned *Old Boy* on and skipped to the tooth part. She wouldn't watch it so I just shrugged and turned up the volume.
I once read that with kids you're supposed to give them a choice. Like if you say Do you want sprouts they say Hell no but if you say You can have ten sprouts or three sprouts they say Three sprouts and they eat them up because they've made the choice. They're in control. The stupid little fuckers think it was *their* idea. So I put on my gloves and take out the claw hammer. This time it's the one you used to kill Izzie, and there's lots of blood still on it which I let your daughter see. Then I say Back or Front and her nostrils kind of flare like a horse and it turns out that giving them a choice doesn't work so well so I just take one of the back ones and tell her that If there's any more funny business et cetera.
Then I realise that she didn't get the message before. So maybe she doesn't really understand now, either, despite the bloody hammer and the tooth. So I go and get your golf bag from upstairs. When she's back with it properly which takes about an hour I take the things out of your bag one at a time and we have

a little chat about what she thinks each one is for and I only have to correct her a few times even though she's having to spit a lot of blood on the floor while we're talking. Then I pack everything away and take her upstairs to the bathroom and I lock her in. There's room in the bath for her to sleep don't worry.

I don't want you to get the wrong impression. I don't just pick on those that deserve it, the sinners, the ungrateful, the high and mighty, the beautiful, the successful the sex workers the hitchhikers the slim girls in jeans with shoulder length hair parted down the middle clutching textbooks to their sweaters the ones that remind me of my father mother dead little sister touchy-feely grandpa. That's not really ever in my mind when I'm choosing. Like that Saramago guy, I just kind of stumble onto them. And I'm definitely not some Robin Hood just going after cunts like you who drive a Mercedes and play golf and drink champagne and wear ties voluntarily.
Far from it.
The best time to hang around Ladbrokes is early afternoon on a Friday when everyone's benefits have been paid out. They get a flush in their faces that I like to watch drain over the next two or three hours as they're gormlessly gaping at the flickering screens and tapping tapping tapping and feeling their pockets get lighter and lighter. Some of them do okay, some of them even break even, but a lot just sit there until they're cleared out and only have a few quid left for a pint or two. Now after a long week of scraping by eating dry bread, drinking Oxo cubes mixed in hot water, and a long session at Ladbrokes those couple of Carlings are looking pretty fucking good to them, and it takes every ounce of willpower for them to not drop those last coins into the machine. That's the red line for them, those gold coins. The final straw. Those four or five gold coins are very damn precious to them, more than any of your fancy wines and chronograph watches and thirty year old whiskies, because they're all that's stopping them from going home cold stone sober to a damp dingy empty council flat with no carpet and no bed just a few blankets on the floor to stare at the outlines on the walls where the furniture used to be.

I hit them from behind and cut open their pockets with a switchblade and take their wallets. I'm wearing a balaclava so I turn them over and I hit them again if they're looking too comfortable. Then I take out the coins from their wallet and I hold them up to their faces and then I make them watch as I lob them as far as I can or just open up my mouth and swallow them down and I grin. If I have time I cut up their tracksuits or find their phone or their roll ups and step on them a few times and then I head off down the alley laughing. The hard part is not to get too carried away but otherwise it's a great way to spend a Friday, it keeps me buzzing nearly all weekend just thinking about their miserable faces.

There's another serial killer I like, a Russian guy, but my internet is a bit flaky today as I'm on the road so I can't go on Wikipedia to check the spelling of his name but I guess it doesn't really matter. I don't mean the one who couldn't get an erection, him I remember, that's the Butcher of Rostov. No this was another one, not very prolific, maybe ten boys total. What's so interesting about this one I hear you ask. Why are you telling me about another serial killer? Just shut the fuck up and read. You might learn something, or maybe I'll throw in something about your dead wife or your kids. You never know. So anyway, this Russian guy, he's big in the community, like a Scout leader or whatever the equivalent is in Soviet Russia. He's got access to a bunch of kids. Obviously he's got a thing for young boys, and there was something to do with an event in his childhood yadda yadda yadda so far so predictable I'm sure he liked stringing up cats and wetting the bed and starting fires and all the usual.
Anyway, he's interesting because he persuades these young boys to go out into the forest with him. There's no abduction, no violence, no coercion. That all comes later. No, every last one of his victims went willingly. He sweet talks them. He says to them, and I'm not kidding, Oh your spine is looking a bit bent, but don't worry kid I know this really good trick to fix that. No its not balloons don't be an idiot. No, he says. Put this noose around your neck that I've hung from this tree and this'll straighten you right out Quasimodo. He says this with a straight face to little

Vovochka. He says You might lose consciousness but don't worry I'll be here and when you wake up that crooked spine will be straight as our Dear General Secretary's prick. And little Vovochka says Sure thing boss what could possibly be strange about that idea just lead the way do you mind if I skip into the deep dark forest with you whistling an innocent tune and our guy just has this twinkle in his eye.

So our Russian serial killer takes them out into the woods, shows them the noose, and they scramble up into it, tighten it around their own necks, THEY TIGHTEN THE HANGMAN'S NOOSE AROUND THEIR OWN NECKS, and he says Oh by the way I brought my camera I hope you don't mind and they smile and say No problem Russian Akela and then he kicks the platform away and they drop and he waits until they're unconscious and then cuts them down and poses their bodies in various positions and masturbates and takes his videos and when he's finished he revives them. The funny thing is, none of them remember it being at all weird and forget to mention it around the samovar that night so he gets away with it again and again and again and again, straightening one crooked back at a time.

Only reviving them gets a bit tame after a while or he just gets a bit carried away so sometimes he doesn't cut them down in time and when they're dead he cuts them up and burns the bodies in the woods and no-one thinks to ask after poor little Vovochka because this is Soviet Russia and missing little boys are the last thing people are worrying about. There's video of this all, by the way. It's on the internet go take a look if you have five minutes. Little Vovochka stepping up onto the platform and putting his head into the noose whilst the serial killer carries on talking about stretching the spine and other bullshit. In one of the videos you see a kid realise what's going on, Oh gee whizz maybe this was a bad idea, and he's kicking out, thrashing around like a fish on a hook, and he manages to get a foot on the tree to support himself but our guy just walks up and holds his legs together until he stops moving then pours petrol on him and burns the body. I guess the moral of the story is don't believe a word a serial killer ever tells you, or just try not to thrash around too much when you're caught in the snare because instead of just being molested and filmed you could end up burned alive in the woods and no-one will ever remember you.

It may surprise you how little I carry around with me. You see all these kids running around with machetes and Mac 10s and Baikals and Zorakis and other weird and wonderful weapons just in case they ever get pulled over for their minor criminal shit and how many of them ever get to use it? Most British cops only have a CS spray and a fucking truncheon, and maybe a taser, and if you get close enough those are pretty useless. Sure they're wearing stab vests but it's easy enough to find the right places and you only need maybe a five centimetre blade, if that. And if it comes down to the big showdown, the final boss fight, it takes maybe three seconds to whip out a small blade and open up your veins to get the job done and if blind people can make themselves coffee and ride trains and cross roads then you can learn to nick an artery even with your ears bleeding from the flashbang or with five plods trying to put you in a headlock. No need for cyanide in false teeth or a C4 belt or a Rambo gun. A few slits, problem solved, enjoy oblivion, your Wikipedia article has practically written itself.

Remember the bit in Se7en where the killer disfigures that woman and tells her she can either call for help or kill herself? It's a great little scene, because you're kind of on the killer's side again. It's the last killing before we finally get to meet John Doe Detective Detective DETECTIVE and it's a quick one, the scene is like a minute long, and the only thing you learn about the dead woman is that she has a big portrait of herself on her wall and she has a prescription for painkillers. The serial killer doesn't even really kill her he just breaks into her house mutilates her face and gives her the choice: call for help and live or overdose on painkillers and die, knowing all along that there is no choice for her at all. She kills herself, because she's a self-centred, conceited, narcissistic, proud, superficial, vain bitch. How horrid her world and her mind must have been to decide that death would be preferable to a life with a destroyed face. This is a woman, a woman so ugly on the inside that she couldn't bear to go on living if she couldn't be beautiful on the outside. She *deserves* to die. She brought it on herself. She's only got herself to blame. She's what's wrong with the world today, she's one of those preening jet-setting perma-tanned starlet models driving around in their Porsche 4x4s dripping with makeup and money and expensive clothes, all style and no substance, more money than sense, more legs than brains. And we're with John Doe here, you can kind of see his point of view, right?

Oh but let me play devil's advocate here for a second. Because it's interesting isn't it, if you look a bit closer. No, this woman isn't proud, or vain. Or, not *especially*. The sin of *pride* certainly isn't why she chose the pills. Think about it. She's just been attacked in her home, in the bath, tied up and then marked by a serial killer, disfigured for life for imaginary sins by a serial killer who cuts off her nose (to spite her face, as Morgan deadpans like a fucking psycho himself). Is she really guilty of *pride* when she chooses the pills?

Imagine yourself lying there on that bed in her place, still shaking from the terror as, naked in the bath, you realised there was an intruder in your home, tasting the blood pouring down the back of your throat, feeling the burn where his hands tied you up, reliving over and over the unforgettable sensation of your nose being carved from your face, remembering that soft hectoring judgmental voice in your ear, feeling the terrible agony as you ooze and swell and writhe, as your sinuses and cartilage and muscles and bones are exposed to the air and your tears sting as they run down your butchered face. Take it from me, I've been there, and I've seen what it does to a person, those final few seconds where they know for sure that they're about to be cut. Even if you manage to blot out the horrifying pain and fight down that desperate reptile desire to stop it hurting, there's plenty of other reasons to chug that bottle of pills, none of which have to do with *pride*. Oh sure, you could be saved, but for the rest of your horrible, painful, hermit life, every morning when you wake up and look in the mirror, you'll see his work, you'll feel his mark of judgment on you, known you were chosen by this crazy person from billions of others to make a stupid point. You'll never feel safe ever again, you'll never be able to take a

bath without a loaded gun next to you, you'll never feel the light caress of a lover on your cheek, never feel *anything* in most of your face again, numb forever beneath all the scar tissue and plastic surgery. And then your husband leaves you and your children are afraid of you and you lose your job and your friends never ever come around and everyone sort of stares at your forehead to avoid looking at the car wreck that is your face and you spend more and more time inside, addicted to painkillers and drinking too much and sobbing into your pillow and longing to be touched loved held again one last time. And when you do force yourself outside, and you walk down the street with your mask on, with your thick makeup and your long hair and someone else's nose stitched to your face and people turn to look at you what is it that you're guilty of is it vanity or pride? Or is it fear loneliness opprobrium rejection abandonment pity pity *pity*. The glare of other people, that look, that look of There's something strange about her and then that second look, so much more devastating than the first, that curious look where they peer a bit closer, maybe stop and turn to watch you walk by, the look of the rubbernecker on the motorway, the look that is wondering Why someone would do that to her, What is wrong with her, What can she have done, and imagine that look every single day of the rest of your life and you really think there's any choice? Is that *pride*? Of course not. It isn't about pride or vanity or conceit at all, not really. She isn't choosing looks over life. It's a choice between a lifetime of crippling punishment shame pain judgment pitying curious stares or a quick, painless death.
You really think you could lie there with your nose or your kids missing and live out the rest of your life in purgatory like that? Of course not. There's no choice at all. John Doe knows that and we know that and now I think you know that, too.

Your daughter lost another tooth today. I was upstairs writing this and she locked the dog in the bathroom and managed to get fifty metres into the woods and it was all a bit *Kiss The Girls* but there are no cliffs for her to jump off and I catch up to her eventually, malnutrition does that to you, and I make sure to tell her that. As well as the tooth I had to use one of the things from your golf bag on her. That'll teach you, won't it? She's lucky I don't just cut her fucking throat to be honest, I've had it up to here with her and it's a good job we're almost done otherwise otherwise otherwise.

I call up not-Marlowe for a chat.
He's an unpleasant guy, a real prick if you want the truth. He doesn't take the hint. I explain it all very carefully to him. I tell him we've got more on you than he can dream of, that we're already hitting you for £5k a month (a lie, sure, but I'm thinking of doing it so if he checks it can be true), and that he should just fuck off and find another mark if he knows what's good for him. When he hangs up on me I have to fight down my first impulse which you can probably guess. Like I said, I have to be careful.
Now maybe you're thinking that's a stupid move. You're thinking if not-Marlowe knows that someone else is already blackmailing you then:
1) you are really dirty
2) you will pay out if pressed
3) someone else is already doing most of the hard work.
These are all reasonable assumptions and not-Marlowe regurgitates these to me in so many words. What I was counting on was not-Marlowe understanding that if someone else is already blackmailing you they've got a rather big incentive to stop other people blackmailing you. That, and I was hoping not-Marlowe would have a bit of professional fucking courtesy. But he's just some thick cunt from Nottingham with dollar signs in his eyes and so I have to hatch another plan.
At first I think that if I can't stop him blackmailing you by blackmailing you first maybe I should blackmail him instead. (The more I think about that the stupider I realise it sounds.)
Then I think that maybe I should just break one of his legs.
Then I think wouldn't it be funny to pin Katee's murder on him but that's complicated and a lot of work and to be honest a massive can of worms.
Then I think that maybe I should just strangle one of his relatives.
Then I think that maybe I should cut off his fingers with piano

wire.
Then I think that maybe I should stitch him into a canvas sack and throw him into the fucking ocean.
Then I realise all I really need to do is give him a bit of a scare so I decide to steal all his money and burn down his house.

You drop your son off at school for the first time in forever. You watch him climb the steps up the school without getting out of the car. Then you drive away, and I frown because you're going the wrong way, you're heading out of town, out of routine. Your calendar doesn't have you going anywhere but work this morning and I begin to sweat a bit. For a while as we're driving I think you've clocked me or you realise I've been[4]

I pop the hinges on not-Marlowe's Burton Eurovault Atlas safe with two blobs of semtex and I take the gold and cash and throw the rest into the stack of furniture in the centre of the room. I pour some more kerosene around before I leave. I light the cigarette and fasten it with a rubber band to the three matches wrapped in a sheet of paper and wedge it under the door which should give me plenty of time to get clear. Did you know that arsonists are amongst the most prolific serial killers? Pretty interesting, huh? But it means that I can't stick around because they sometimes take photographs of the gaggle of gawping neighbours to catch familiar faces. I read online the next day that not-Marlowe's mother was living in a granny flat above the garage but I don't think she suffered much and I may or may not have checked that part of the house and may or may not have accidentally suffocated her with a pillow before I lit the fire, you know what they say, accidents happen.
I did you a favour. Not-Marlowe backs right off after that.

Talking of fire, you've probably heard of this old Indian custom where the widow jumps on the funeral pyre to be with her dear departed in the afterlife. It's called sati, and we British of all fucking people stopped them doing it, though why we cared

---

[4] EN: The author left this sentence finished in the original document.

about the lives of fifty-year-old Indian women who the fuck knows, maybe they produced a lot of cloth or whatever. Anyway these women are really upset about their husbands being dead and they don't have much chance of getting another one, so into the fire they skip, because that's always the best solution for everything, right? Burn it with fire.
Only it doesn't always work out like they're hoping.
Because you see what seems like a really good idea at the time changes pretty fucking quickly when you feel the flames tickling your feet or the pool filter prolapsing your anus. Funny that. But these Indians like a good show so they say Are you sure about this Mrs Singh and she pulls herself up all dignified like and says Of course and they smile at one another and say Well if you insist so they build the fire extra big and they say again Are you really sure about this Mrs Singh and she's all Yes and they say OK but to be really sure we'll have to tie you down and Mrs Singh is like I'll be fine I don't need any tying down I just want to be with my hubby and they look at one another and they say But really Mrs Singh we must insist and she shrugs and says Fine, Whatever, and puts on her Noble face and lets them tie her to the pile of wood next to Mr Singh's bloated body.
Because they know, they know, they know. They've seen the ones that jump into the fire pit all gung ho and then really really really regret the decision when they start to turn a bit crispy. They've heard the shrieking and seen the clawing and the panic and the fear and the terrible curses. They've watched the smouldering blackened burned bodies crawling out from the flames. They understand what happens. It's that sudden clarity again, that diamond bullet in the forehead, but this time it's like right after you've cummed and you look around and remember what and who and where you've been putting your dick and it hits you What the fucking fuck was I thinking only instead of just wiping yourself off and walking out the door your hair is on fire and your lungs are turning to cinders and your eyes are melting and Mr Singh can rot in hell that fucking potbellied cunt and fuck you all and fuck you for tying me down because you knew you knew *you knew*.

One night with Magnus and me isn't enough for Izzie. She's caught the bug, hard. Looking into those deep blue eyes for hours on end has broken something in your wife, something that can't be fixed, and she needs more.

I'm going to give you a way out. No tricks, this time, I promise; this is legitimate.
In July 1997 Thailand's central bank floated the baht, kicking off the Asian Financial Crisis. The world was on the brink of recession within a year. Of course, that's not exactly the way it happened. The devaluation of the baht wasn't the only reason, I mean. That's like saying a guy named Gav started World War I, or you reading Izzie's diary was the reason you split her head open. There was a backstory, right? Camels and straws and all that.
Anyway, sixteen months after the flotation of the baht, East Asia is totally fucked. This was all in your *Economist* you pretend to read. People lose everything, and just like every time people find their bank accounts empty and their children hungry and the wolf at the door they decide it's time to clock out. People are jumping in front of trains and out windows and off bridges left right and centre. It's mayhem.
Then this woman in Hong Kong has a nifty idea. She's a clever one, with a background in chemistry, and she comes up with this easy and painless and private technique to kill yourself. Now, when you've just lost your job life savings hope apartment, discovering a painless way to end it all begins to sound pretty good. If war is the mother of invention then recession is the father. That's a terrible analogy but it's late and I've had too many drinks and I've just had another session with your daughter and you catch my drift.
This method, it's pretty unusual. Your first reaction when you hear it is What? Does that really work? So of course the press hear of this, report on it, and suddenly everyone is doing it, and it spreads like wildfire.
Maybe one in a hundred people topped themselves using our cheerless chemist's technique when the baht was floated (in the Bank of Thailand's defence, they did it unwillingly, under duress,

after being assailed by international speculators, but I guess you don't really give a shit either way). Just two months after our chemistry grad tops herself it becomes the third most popular method of suicide in Hong Kong. Soon desperate people all over East Asia are shuffling off using this trendy new method.

Before I tell you how she did it why do you reckon people choose *not* to commit suicide? Have a think. For almost everyone it's the pain. They're scared it's going to hurt. Quite common. Everyone is squeamish about their own death. But there are other factors at play here as well. A lot of people are frightened of judgment in the afterlife. Some are petrified about messing it up, waking up in a hospital bed as a vegetable or worse, alive, disfigured, yet another failure. Others are just spooked about the preparation it takes, the fuss of it all, or the burden they'll be, even after death. They're thinking of the poor sap who has to clear up the mess, the kids' PTSD when they find their pa hanging in the shed, the commuters they're going to make late, the dog walker who has to retrieve the rotting hand from Fido's mouth.

So if someone told you about a painless way of doing it in the privacy and comfort of your own home that won't inconvenience anyone, there's no blood, no splatter, no mess, no noise, no disfigurement, even plenty of time to back out if you decide to give life another chance? Your ears are perking up. Now you're thinking Oh sure it'll be a load of drugs that nobody can get hold of and you have to be a chemistry PhD to mix together and you could still wake up a vegetable but let me stop you right there. No drugs. Common household goods. And nothing difficult at all, in fact really bloody simple, a three-year-old could do it. And you're still suspicious. You're thinking Bleach, but like I said, no pain. Okay, you think, Hanging? No, remember, this is one you can stop anytime you like. No hemlock no warm bath no razor blades no plastic bags no gas ovens. So now maybe you're stumped. Give up?

Fucking *barbecues.*

Genius, huh?

So here's what you do.

You go to Tesco. You buy a big bag of charcoal and a barbecue. If you're skint then just five or six of those small disposable ones should do the trick, but even with all the blackmail you've still got enough dough to buy a bag of charcoal and a cheap barbecue and the more charcoal the better really. Then you drive home and take your purchases into your bathroom with a box of matches and a few beverages and a novel or magazine of your choice. Then you write your suicide letter and maybe a big DO NOT ENTER sign and with a few skull and crossbones if your sketching skills are up to it. Tape that to the outside of the door. Close and lock the door behind you and put a rolled up towel along the bottom of it. If you're worried about discovery just wedge a chair under the door handle, but in your case there's no need to bother. Then you take another towel and put it around the edges of the window. You see where we're going here. We're trying to get a nice seal. If you've got one of those extractor fan things you'll need to tape another towel over that, too. Then run a bath, light the charcoal barbecue, take a few sips of your martini whisky vodka coke whatever and settle back into the bath, crack open your novel, and read and drink and soak until you slip into a coma and then die without ever knowing what hit you.

Who knows? Maybe you'll even start a trend.

But before you go running off for the bags of charcoal and put on your robes and crown let me just run you through what will happen if you do wind up dead in your bathtub.

First of all I will remove every tooth from your daughter's mouth.

Then I will skin her arms and legs with a potato peeler, and remove her tongue with a pair of dull scissors.

Then I will open your golf bag and use your tools on her until she doesn't remember a life before me.

Next up I will crack every joint and pop every knuckle in your son's body with a pair of pliers, poke holes in his eyes with a needle, and lock him in a room with Izzie's remains until he starves to death.

Then I will take him out and feed him to your daughter.

Then I will take your mutilated cannibal molested daughter cut off her head and throw her body in the ocean and boil the flesh from her skull and spray paint it gold and put a Fleshlight in the toothless mouth and fuck it for the rest of my life.

Then, to top it all off, I will release every compromising picture, every shred of evidence of your infidelity, your sexual perversions, your role in Izzie's murder, and upload child porn and bestiality videos and anti-Semitic rants and incest novelettes and written fantasies about sucking off your father-in-law and as much fucked up 4chan shit you can possibly imagine to your computer and every public internet profile you own.

Then I will start this all over again with your brother and his family.

5.

Still with me? Okay, good. Almost there now. Chin up.

The police pull you in again. They don't offer you a cup of tea this time. We'd like to go back over a few things. Some of the details don't quite add up. Ha ha. No shit. My efforts are starting to unravel. I've spread too much confusion, and it's starting to look rather strongly like someone is trying to cover up something. They've pulled the ATM cameras and the phone records, combed the footage from the railway station, found her Audi, checked her GPS. What man can invent another can discover. They're asking questions you can't answer, won't answer, daren't answer. There's talk of solicitors. You're starting to feel the noose tighten. It's not quite enough to charge you, but it's getting close, and you know it. You can sense them closing in, pressing down on you, feel the ground underneath you beginning to shift, your grip starting to slip. You probably have a week, maybe two, if you're lucky. The media are starting to sniff about, too.
You can't save yourself, but you can save your kids. That's all you have left now.

Izzie is close to tears. She's sitting on the armchair across from me and refusing to look my way. I take a long drag on my cigarette, taking care to blow the smoke in her direction. That makes her look up, a disgusted look on her face that she does her best to hide. She still needs me, after all. I watch her closely. I see her make the decision. I can pinpoint the exact moment. Nothing else has worked. She's been trying for weeks, and she's desperate. This is the last thing she can think of. The only way she can get Magnus back into her life, even for a moment, for one last hit of those blue eyes, one last suck on that Adonis' cock.
She pulls her hair up into a ponytail in one quick efficient movement. Then she removes her jacket, places it over the arm of the chair, and stands up a little uncertainly. As she walks over

to me she's reaching one hand behind her back to unfasten her bra. I sit almost motionless, spreading my legs just slightly as encouragement. She stands over me for a second looking down, then places one hand on my knee. I can see every little nuance of her face, and I smile. She completely misunderstands. She gets down on her knees, sliding her hand up my thigh. Her other hand reaches for my fly, which she tugs down expertly. She licks her lips and burrows her hand into my jeans, through the gap in my boxers, and grips my penis, which is still flaccid. This seems to perplex her. She caresses it for a moment, then starts jerking it, her cold hands flexing and grasping, vainly and desperately trying to rouse me.
I'm totally uninterested.
I lean forward and whisper into her ear. After about ten seconds she tries to pull away, but I grab her by the wrist, my other hand like a python around her throat. Her hand is still on my cock, which grows bigger as I'm talking. When I'm finished I let her go and she leaps away from me, her face contorted. I wonder for a moment if she'll run, but she can't. I've said precisely the right thing. Her jaw is clenched tight and her chin is wobbling and then she's off, she's collapsed on the floor, wailing and snivelling and retching. I stub out my cigarette on the arm of the sofa and stand up slowly. She doesn't pay any attention to me. Everything is still sinking in. I walk over to her and watch your poor wife curled up on the floor, bawling her eyes out like a toddler, her thighs pulled up tightly against her tits, her hair wild, her expensive clothes dishevelled, her makeup running down her scarlet cheeks, and I pull out my cock and piss on her for a good minute or so. She's too far gone to react. I light another cigarette and walk out the door back home to watch you and the kids for the rest of the night as your whore of a wife tries to scrub the smell of urine shame fear from her hair.

In the book Cape Fear the husband, fed up of trying to get the police to take him seriously, has his family's stalker beaten up by some local toughs. Only it turns out the stalker is a mean sonofabitch, and even though he's outnumbered and takes a bit of a beating he manages to fuck the husband's hired goons up pretty badly, and they only manage to put the stalker out of action with a month of jail time. After that, the husband is on his own. He's got no-one to turn to. The police aren't interested, there's no more goons, and it's between him and his stalker now. And now the clock is ticking, the days whizz by, and every minute of every day the stalker's closer and closer to walking out of prison and coming after him. The husband can't do anything. He's powerless, and he knows it.

He thinks about running but that's no good. The stalker is ruthless, determined, unstoppable. He counts down the days, he obsesses about it, wonders how the fuck he can save his family from this relentless psycho, this man he knows will stop at nothing until he decides it's finished. He tries to live a normal life, but he can't do it, can't put the danger on the horizon out of his mind. What do you do in a situation like that? He's American, so he buys a gun. But what would you do? Buy a cricket bat? A carving knife? No, of course not, you're more likely to get yourself stabbed with the thing. No, there's nothing you can do but wait and see, and hope and pray that the stalker fucks up, or better yet, gives up, moves on, finds another toy.

That waiting, that looking around every corner, that never being able to sleep without one eye open, that dread? That'll be your life if you try to run. And we both know you won't get far with me on your tail. I'll catch up to you eventually.

But how can I trust you?

Oh, we get that question a lot in my line of work. You don't get to ask, I'm afraid. You gave that up when you murdered Izzie. You just have to hope. You have to weigh up your options. I've told you what happens if you try to run. I've told you what happens if you decide to end it all yourself. Now here's what happens if you decide to play games with me.

If you turn yourself in I will arrange so that when the police find your son's corpse they will also find your fluids in places those fluids should never be. I think we both know I can make that happen. Chloe Josie sent me five sticky condoms full from your liaisons with her in those glamorous hotel rooms. Pretty gross, right? But really fucking useful. You never know when a man's

spunk can come in useful. Even if you show this to the police and they somehow believe you and only charge you with Izzie's murder, I will make sure the location of those fluids is extremely well publicised.
And everyone knows what they do to child fuckers in prison.

I realise you're still holding out hope that you'll get to see your kids again. It's understandable. They're all you have left. But it's making you misunderstand the deal here. You're labouring under a false hope, as they say. I want to make it absolutely clear that there is no ending to this that involves you being reunited with them. I know that I can't dispel this fantasy of yours, and there's probably nothing I can say to make you drop the idea. So this morning after breakfast I took your son out for a little road trip (your daughter wasn't quite feeling herself).
It's not far to the other cottage, maybe an hour or so. I can tell he's nervous but he's not pissed himself yet which I guess you could call progress. When I unlock the door and go into the house he loiters outside, reluctant to follow me into the dark. The cottage has that musty smell of old newspapers and damp walls. I switch on the light and tell him to come inside. I walk across to the room and I get out the keys and I start unlocking all the padlocks. Before I pull open the heavy door I turn around and say I'm sorry to have to show you this but it's for the best you deserve to know. Then I put on my mask and tug open the door and I have to use both hands because the thing is really fucking heavy and even through the mask I can smell Izzie and your son turns white and just stands there rooted to the spot. The room is only small and there's no light so I find my torch and pick out Izzie's bloated face with the beam and make sure your son sees it. I'm not sure he quite understands so I explain and point out the parts with the torch. He's sick on the floor and I see the baked beans we had for breakfast, which makes me laugh. After he cleans the sick up I close the door again and we go back outside for a bit of fresh air. Then I tell him what happened to Izzie. I can see he doesn't quite believe me, however much he might hate despise loathe resent you he can't believe *that*. So I show him the pictures (oh yes, I guess I forgot to mention the

pictures. You caught me off guard at the hotel but I always have my camera with me. I carry it everywhere. It's just as essential to my work as my knife or my laptop or my gloves.) Even though your face is a bit blurry he recognises his old man just fine, and the ones where you're dragging her from the rhododendron into the back of your car come out crystal clear anyway.

Now don't get me wrong I didn't traumatise your boy just for the fun of it. I did it so you'll finally realise you'll never see your kids again. Even if God strikes me down for my sins and the dog doesn't tear out their guts when they escape those kids will never want to see your fucking face ever again. I can absolutely guarantee that.

One unfortunate side effect of our little road trip is that your son just straight stops talking to me. I do overhear him whispering something to your daughter at dinner that evening, though, and the way she looks at me the next morning when I come in to untie her I figure he's managed to give her the gist. It's a shame because two uncooperative kids makes my life much more difficult. I decide to move up the deadline a little, which means the end is a bit closer for you. Never mind. I guess that also means I'm going to have to wrap writing this up sooner than I wanted to but we'll see. I might be able to get it done before the fun really starts if I really knuckle down.

Did you realise you'd been duped when you found Izzie alone in the hotel, smoking on the balcony and not fucking someone else between the sheets? You could have walked away. She never heard you come in. You could have crept away and that was it, she would never have known. But I guess the reptile part of your brain had taken over by then, because that second hammer blow didn't strike me as the product of level-headed rational human decision-making. That first hammer blow was primate anger jealousy rage, but that second one? That second one was cold. That second one was revenge. That second one was all reptile.

Oh, how wrong you were. If only you'd stopped to think for once in your stupid little life. Izzie was never at the hotel to cuckold you. Izzie was at that hotel to *protect* you.

Since that night where she tried to blow me to get access to Magnus one last time, I had managed to convince Izzie that you were in serious shit, and that trouble was about to boil over everyone around you. I showed her the videos of you and Katee, I showed her the videos of you and Josie, and then I showed her your bank statements. Then I explained. It didn't take long to make her understand. Most of it was lies, sure, but there was plenty of hard evidence sitting in front of her to make the fibs seem more than plausible. By then she didn't exactly hold you in high esteem, and it was pretty easy to convince her that you were a dirty fucking slimeball, if she needed any convincing at all.

Anyway, she completely bought the idea that that I was blackmailing you. I explained that you were starting to get a bit stroppy about paying up. I told her some war stories about how my organisation worked when our revenue stream was threatened. How we sometimes had to resort to some unpleasant methods, and gave her some pertinent examples where, after applying the right amount of force against vulnerable parts of the mark's life, usually immediate family, the payments tended to get back on track pretty promptly. I told her that little Gladiator story about Paolo's wife and kid, as well as some others. Izzie was a clever woman. She understood how my business worked. I told her how foolish you were being. I convinced her that even if she took the kids and ran how easy it would be to find her, and made it crystal clear what would happen if she tried to contact the police, which a few facts about her daily routine and passwords and the addresses of her parents and sister and a detailed narrative of her schedule for the upcoming week and the name of your daughter's closest friends seemed to really drive home. Knowledge really is power in my line of work, and I really had quite a lot of it to wield by then.

Izzie was expecting a phone call off me that night in the hotel. We were going to discuss ways she could delay me hurting her children. We were going to talk about payment schedules. She was going to do a deal, the most important one of her life. She was in that room to protect her family, not to fuck Magnus or me or some imaginary John Jack Jim. You killed your wife just as she was trying to save her children from the sins and stupidity of their father.

Now of course we both know that it was just another game for me. But Izzie didn't know that. That's really important to remember. *Izzie did not know I wasn't completely serious.* She honestly believed her family were in real mortal danger (which I guess was true). Izzie came to that hotel room, alone, unarmed, at the request of someone who had manipulated her into having unprotected vaginal and anal sex, threatened the lives of her children, her parents, and her sister, and explained in harrowing detail what would happen to her family if she didn't cooperate. She was in that hotel room trying to stop me. She was in that hotel room to save her family from you. And you killed her for it. Pretty ironic, huh? How petty your jealous rage must seem now. How childish, how *selfish*.

The reason Ted Bundy is my all time favourite serial killer is because he's so fucking *lucky*. He drives around in the same fucking car everywhere. Witnesses fail to pick him out of lineups. He goes back repeatedly to crime scenes, carries weapons and other murder paraphernalia around with him in his car, takes tokens from victims, makes threats to people who know him, allows victims to escape. He thinks he's charismatic and good-looking, but he's neither. Four or five different people recognise him from a profile the police put out, report him, and yet the police ignore him as a suspect. He escapes prison not once, but twice.
Twice.
But aside from that luck, what always got me was the *stories*. Bundy was a clever guy. He had an IQ of 136. But he used terrible, terrible props and told terrible, terrible stories and WOMEN STILL WENT WITH HIM. They followed him off the path, down the alley, away from the light, into the VW beetle, like he's the fucking Pied Piper of Hamlin. He approached five women in broad daylight, introduced himself as Ted, and said he needed help unloading a sailboat and he DIDN'T EVEN HAVE A SAILBOAT. One of the women goes with him, and runs away

when she realises there is no sailboat. So what does he do? HE IMMEDIATELY TRIES THE STORY ON ANOTHER WOMAN. And it worked. She followed him. She's dead. Bundy's a fucking chancer, but he's got balls. YOU'VE GOT THE TERRIBLE SHRINKS. I mean, to be like that, to not give a shit, to be so fucking casual and brazenly obvious about something like kidnap and rape and murder? That always impressed me.

He tells them awful lies and they follow him into the darkness anyway. It's almost like they want to believe him. It's almost like they want to believe him. It's almost like they want to follow him into the darkness and they want to believe him.

I've left a passworded file on your desktop called AMONTILLADO. The password is the name of Nashe's young friend followed by the amount of cash you handed me when you crashed into the back of me followed by Mr Twit's miracle cure for Mrs Twit so it's a good job you didn't skip right to this part isn't it? The file contains the location of the cottage, saved as a Bookmark X. Fifteen men on a dead man's chest et cetera.

You will go to the cottage at midday on your son's birthday.

When you arrive at the cottage you will wait in your car for one hour. Once the hour is up, you will get out of the car, and leave all of your personal belongings on the bonnet. Phone, wallet, watch et cetera. You will then proceed into the cottage, via the front door, which I've left unlocked. You will walk five steps into the house and turn left. In front of you will be a large, heavy door, locked with two deadbolts and a latch. Withdraw the deadbolts and open the door. Walk inside. The smell will be awful, but you are not permitted to bring a mask or cover your face in any way. I have cameras throughout the house, and I will be watching. Pull the door closed behind you. It will lock automatically.

I don't need to threaten you. I don't need to explain to you the importance of following my instructions precisely, without deviation, without hesitation, without any fucking around. I am watching you. Any hint of misbehaviour, well, I think this note makes everything quite clear, don't you? You should understand by now what will happen to your children if you do not walk into my box. You should understand what will happen to *you* if you do not walk into my box. There really is no other option for you.

Immurement. That's the name of it. No, not immolation. That's burning. Immurement is the act of encumbering or encompassing or enclosing, usually within walls. It's not a particularly popular form of execution. It lacks the gore of a beheading, the spectacle of a crucifixion, the dazzle of a burning at the stake, the frisson of a hanging. It's a slow death. It takes time. Hours, days, weeks even. The end is prolonged. There's not even all that much suffering. You brick them up behind a wall, or maybe stuff them in a box and close the lid on them. It's all very private, very little mess, very few screams.
So what's the attraction?
Well there's a couple of reasons.
Historically, immurements have been methods of sacrifice, and only rarely used as punishment. Don't want your bridge temple pyramid to collapse? Brick up a few slaves in the walls, that'll appease the gods. Their deaths are valuable, they are buying something, a trade of a few lives to ensure the greatness longevity prosperity of the civilization. There's something noble about sacrifice like that, whether it's voluntary or not. I like the idea of you sacrificing yourself to me in exchange for the lives of your children.
The other reason I like it is because it takes away all the glamour away from the killing. It's boring. It's simple. One stone at a time. There's no spectacle. By the end of the first week everyone will have forgotten all about it, even quicker if they victim is bricked up in a wall. How quickly we move on with our lives. But the victim has to live every minute. He's not in much pain. Depending on how much room he's got there might be some discomfort, some sores, some unpleasant smells, but except towards the end he's not really in any physical pain. No, all the pain is in his own head, of his own making. His imagination is the real torture, his thoughts his real suffering, time and its inexorable, relentless passage his real enemy, not the executioner's blade or needle or noose. *The perceived hollow.* Slowly, slowly, slowly, as he weakens, as he feels the end nearing, his stomach eating itself, he really understands, and he

finally accepts his fate.

You'll probably last about a week, maybe ten days. The room isn't air tight. Now, you're going to get hungry first. Whatever you do, don't even think about eating any of Izzie's remains. She's just too far gone for that. You don't want to spend the last hours of your life shitting out your guts with the taste of Izzie's rotting flesh on your lips. Wikipedia says terminal dehydration is a peaceful way to go, all things considered. You'll be a bit dizzy, a little light-headed, but other than that you'll drift off pretty quietly, if you can get used to the dark and the smell. If the idea makes you a bit nervous just remember the alternatives, and man the fuck up.

There's an old Tamil ritual called vatakkiruttal. Grand old kings defeated in battle or disgraced in some way would regain their honour by walling themselves up in caves with their followers and starving themselves to death whilst facing north. The people wrote songs and poems about these noble kings and their self-sacrifice, their resolution, their strength of will, their selflessness. These were brave men who had no other choice, and they marched to their deaths with their heads held high.
The wall opposite the door faces north, if you're interested.

La fatal pietra sovra me si chiuse.
Ecco la tomba mia. Del dì la luce
Più non vedrò.[5]

---

[5]EN: "The fatal stone upon me now is closing,
Now has the tomb engulfed me. I never more
The light shall behold." Verdi, Aida (1893), Act IV, Scene III

Second Document

Poor Radames! Poor Fortunato! Poor Ugolino! Poor Antigone! Poor Livilla! And they in misery, miserable fate/ Lamenting, waste away.

You are such a fucking moron. I CANNOT BELIEVE THAT WORKED. Did you not read that part about Bundy? How could you think that this would end well for you? There is no such thing as redemption. You will not be saved. Your shame will not be expunged. You will rot in there. It will be agony. The world will still know who you are and what you did, and you will have achieved nothing. *Nothing*.

You made two mistakes.

First of all, there were no cameras. Of course there weren't. You think I'd want to miss this? I was sitting upstairs the whole time. I still am. I could hear you walking around for ages before you went in. You really should have come upstairs. We could have had a proper boss fight, I could even have obliged and cackled maniacally and monologued as your love for your kids gives you the strength of ten men and you could have wrung the life out of me, you emerging victorious, the hero of the story. Never mind.

Secondly, you should have looked a bit more closely at Izzie's remains. Maybe counted the heads before you pulled that door shut behind you. I'll wait. I know its pretty dark in there. Take your time. Have a feel around. Oh, what's that? *Two* heads? Now I wonder who could that be? Did you notice how the smallest of the two is missing all its teeth? Maybe you should bring it closer to the light. Or not. You've got plenty of time to decide. The father ate a sour grape, and his children's teeth are set on edge. Or just pulled out with a claw hammer.

Actually, three. You made three mistakes. You should not have believed a word I wrote.

Poor green eyes. Tu... in questa tomba![6]

I have your son here with me. Yes, right here upstairs. Now I know what you're thinking. How do I know that? How do I know you haven't just killed him you fucking pig monster? But you'll recognise his screams, right? Every good father knows what his kid's screams sounds like.

That dripping? Intentional. No it won't go away. Yes I know you could drink it. It might or might not be your son's blood. I think I can keep him alive for at least three or four days if I'm careful with the cuts. Yes you'll live for a little longer. Yes you will still starve to death. No this does not end well for you. No your children will not survive you. No you will not get out of that room alive. Yes it will hurt.

Scream away, Fortunato, pound the walls, rend your hair, claw your face, writhe around on that hook as much as you like. It only makes me smile all the more.

---

[6]EN: "You... with me here buried!" Verdi, *Aida* (1893), Act IV, Scene III

Editor's Afterword

The two documents that comprise this narrative were recovered from the crime scene of a family annihilation, or murder-suicide.

The first document was the only file found on a badly damaged USB stick in the father's shoe. The second document was handwritten in block capitals on three sides of notepad paper, and was also hidden at the crime scene. From the contents and tone of the documents, one must assume that the authors were one and the same, although like many aspects of this case, this remains unproven.

I have divided the first document into numbered sections and made some minor typographical edits throughout this narrative for the purpose of clarity, as well as changing names, places, and dates to preserve the privacy of the victims' family, who, like the police, consider this case closed. I have tried to retain as much of the original grammar and punctuation as possible to ensure the tone of the narrative remains intact. More obtrusively, and after considerable reflection, I removed a lengthy discussion of the mutilation of a man and an act of molesting a minor from the first document for being too disturbing for publication.

It was nearly two years between the family's disappearance and the discovery of their bodies - the husband, wife, and their two children - in a derelict holiday cottage in the Cotswolds. As a result, the second handwritten document was water-damaged, resulting in the complete loss of the seventh and eighth paragraphs. I have managed to piece together the remains of the document and reproduce them here as best I can.

As in the first document, I removed three extremely graphic sentences, which elaborate on the supposed fate of the son that was neither supported nor disproved by the forensic evidence; the bodies were in an extremely advanced state of decomposition when discovered, and the descriptions of torture cannot be proven conclusively as most of the children's remains were missing from the crime scene.

For these changes, redactions, and omissions, and for what I have decided to keep intact, I take full and sole responsibility.

The authenticity of these documents and their contents has never been proven. The authorities believe both documents to be a hoax, authored by the paranoid and possibly disturbed father. The father remains the sole suspect for the murder-suicide of his family, despite the claims made in these documents, and the significant efforts made by others and myself to overturn this verdict.

These documents were, of course, untitled. The title I have chosen is from Shakespeare, and, I hope, apt:

O villain, villain, smiling, damnèd villain!
My tables!—Meet it is I set it down
That one may smile, and smile, and be a villain.
Shakespeare, *Hamlet*, Act I, Scene V

Alex Berkman
Editor
Inverness, Scotland

Printed in Great Britain
by Amazon